MURDER
ON PAY DAY

A heist, a killing, and dangerous
criminals at large in the west of Ireland

DAVID PEARSON

THE
BOOK
FOLKS

Paperback edition published by

The Book Folks

London, 2018

© David Pearson

This book is a work of fiction. Names, characters, businesses, organizations, places and events are either the product of the author's imagination or are used fictitiously. Any resemblance to actual persons, living or dead, events or locales is entirely coincidental. The spelling is British English.

ISBN 978-1-7287-6934-9

www.thebookfolks.com

To Harry, for being a caring and generous friend.

Chapter One

Garda Pascal Brosnan finished his breakfast in the kitchen of his modest bungalow which was situated just a few hundred metres from the small Garda station that he ran single-handedly at the edge of the village of Roundstone in Connemara.

It was a cold December morning, and he knew that the windows of his car would probably be covered in a thin layer of frost, so when he had put on his uniform jacket, he filled a large plastic jug with warm water from the electric kettle, checked that the house was secure and left by the front door.

He had been right about the car. The windows were indeed covered in ice, so he gently poured the warm water on the front windscreen, side and back windows, dispersing the obstruction and leaving the glass clear.

He arrived at the Garda station a few minutes later. Today was pay day for the entire Irish police force. They weren't usually paid until the last Friday of the month, but in December, payment was made early to allow people to fund what seemed like the ever-increasing cost of Christmas.

When Brosnan had turned on the electric heaters in the small building, he powered up the station's single computer, and went to put the kettle on while the rather old PC got itself ready for work.

When he had checked the overnight bulletins from Galway, Clifden and headquarters in Dublin, none of which thankfully affected him directly in the quiet backwater that made up his patch, he logged onto his own personal on-line bank account.

"Nice one," he said to himself. Not only had his salary been deposited for him, but he had also been reimbursed for an amount of necessary expenditure that he had paid for out of his own pocket in the preceding months.

Brosnan would now be able to travel into Galway at the weekend and buy the small number of Christmas gifts for his immediate family, with whom he would spend the day on the 25th. His parents were still alive and well, living in a small terraced house in the city; his brother and sister would be there too, which was about the only time Brosnan got to see the rest of the family for the whole year. His father, now retired, had worked his whole life on the docks in Galway as a stevedore, and had retired at the age of sixty-two when those jobs came to an end. The work had provided his family with modest, but adequate means, and the three children had been brought up in a very traditional, caring manner.

Pascal had joined the Garda Síochána as soon as he left school, and had spent most of his career to date working initially out of Galway city's Mill Street station, then later in Clifden, before volunteering to take on the station in Roundstone. It could be a solitary existence, but he could call on backup from Sergeant Séan Mulholland and his team in Clifden, when required, and despite the fact that Roundstone was a small village, there was a surprisingly vibrant social life, which Brosnan exploited to the full.

He was going through a rudimentary shopping list in his head, when the door to the station opened, and one of the old timers from the area came in.

"Hello Aongus, you're out early. What can I do for you?" Brosnan asked.

"God, I'm after having a right shock, Pascal. I was out for a walk across on the headland with Texas, when he took off like a mad thing. I eventually caught up with him, and he was sniffing around something that had washed up on the rocks. There was an awful smell – it was putrefied, and that's for sure," the old man said.

"I see. So, what do you think it was then, Aongus?" Brosnan asked.

"That's just it, Pascal. It's a body!" the old man said, clearly upset by the event.

"Are you sure, Aongus? A body you say."

"I am that. It's a body all right," Aongus said.

"God help us. Well I'd better come and have a look. Can you show me where you found it?" Brosnan said, reaching for his overcoat and peaked cap.

The two men got into Brosnan's car, and drove down the track leading to the headland till it came to an end where Brosnan parked.

They walked out across the stumpy grass till they got near the end of the promontory where there was an almost sheer drop onto the rocks and the sea below. Brosnan

3

could smell the undeniable stench of rotting flesh from the top where he stood, and far below, lodged in the craggy terrain, he could make out the twisted form of what had once been a living thing, now blackened by exposure to the elements.

Aongus gagged on seeing the body for a second time, and told Brosnan he was going back into town to get a glass of whisky to settle his stomach.

"Fair enough, Aongus. But you'll have to come back in to me later to make a statement. I'll have to get the detectives out from Galway to deal with this. Dead bodies are way above my pay grade."

* * *

Inspector Maureen Lyons was busy completing the monthly reports on crime in Galway for November when her phone rang. She disliked paperwork intensely, but it was becoming a more prominent feature of policing of late, and her ultimate senior officer, Superintendent Finbarr Plunkett was very unforgiving if these reports weren't submitted on time. She would much prefer to be out catching thieves than sitting in the office, even in the cold weather.

"Lyons," she said.

"Hello, Inspector. This is Pascal Brosnan out in Roundstone. One of the locals has found a body out here on the headland, I'm out there now. I need some backup and all the usual," Brosnan said in as near to an excited voice as the usually placid man could manage.

"Take it easy Pascal, it will be fine. Now where exactly is this body, and do you know if it's male or female, clothed or naked, or anything else about it?"

4

"I can't get down to it, Inspector, it's on the rocks out here. All I can tell you is that it's in an advanced state of decay. It smells awful, and it's all black. What do you want me to do?"

"Well, stay there in any case. Can you cordon off the area? I have to meet Superintendent Plunkett in half an hour, but I'll get Eamon and Sally out to you. Have you told Sergeant Mulholland?" Lyons asked.

"No, not yet, I called you first," Brosnan said, calming down a little now that he had some moral support.

"OK. Well, call him as soon as we're finished here and he'll be able to get someone out to you as well. It will take Eamon forty-five minutes to get there. And try and preserve the site as best you can, Pascal. OK? Before you go, Pascal, does it look like natural causes – like maybe someone just slipped off the high ground?" she said.

"God, I don't know. There's been no one reported missing recently, though I suppose it could have been a tourist," Brosnan said.

"Hardly, at this time of year, Pascal. But I suppose you never know. Oh, and can you text me the co-ordinates of the location so I can give Eamon proper directions," Lyons said.

"Right, no bother. Anyway, I'll wait here and make sure no one interferes with it till backup arrives," Brosnan said.

"Just what we bloody need, this week of all weeks," Lyons said to herself as she went to find Eamon Flynn and Sally Fahy to get them moving.

Chapter Two

Sergeant Séan Mulholland had just put the kettle on for the first of his morning cups of tea when the phone rang. He had opened the Garda Station at 9 a.m. as usual, and was glad to get in out of the weather. The thin north westerly breeze was making it feel a lot colder on the streets of the small town than the actual temperature warranted.

Mulholland was in his late fifties, and could have retired earlier from the force, but had elected to stay on for a few more years. He was a confirmed bachelor, and had few interests other than his work, and a bit of coarse fishing on any of the many lakes that surrounded the town. While not universally liked by everyone in Clifden, he was known to be a fair man, and would often overlook small demeanours rather than get involved in masses of paperwork to prosecute someone who had failed to renew their shotgun license on time, or hadn't taxed their car or van at the appropriate time.

The station had a total of eleven Gardaí assigned to it, so there were generally three officers and Mulholland on duty at any time once shift patterns, holidays, training and other forms of leave had been taken into account.

Mulholland took the call from Brosnan who had calmed down a bit since his first call with Lyons. Brosnan explained what had been discovered.

"You'll have to stay there a while, Pascal," Mulholland said, "Jim Dolan is away out at Clifden Glen with the car just now – there's some talk of a break in overnight. But I'll get him out to you as soon as I can. The folks from Galway will probably get there first. It's a bad time of year for someone to end up like that," Mulholland said.

* * *

Detective Sergeant Eamon Flynn and Detective Garda Sally Fahy set off with sirens and flashing lights at high speed towards Clifden. Sally Fahy was the youngest detective in Hays' team. She had started out as a civilian worker helping the team with paperwork a few years ago, and enjoyed it so much that Maureen Lyons had little trouble in persuading her to apply for a post in the force. Sally had excelled during her training at Templemore, and when she had passed out, Hays pulled in a few favours and got her assigned to his unit in Galway. Sally had proved to be a very useful member of the team, and she got on well with the rest of them, which was an added bonus.

They had been briefed by Inspector Lyons about the discovery out at Roundstone, and both were keen to demonstrate that they were up to the task in hand with promotions in the offing. They arrived in Roundstone some forty minutes after leaving Galway, and went screaming through the little village, much to the amazement of the locals who were just getting up and about at ten-thirty in the morning.

They managed to get the car out onto the grass down at the end of the track leading to the magnificent beach at Dog's Bay, and drove as quickly as they dared to where Pascal Brosnan was standing at the end of the peninsula.

"God, that was quick," Brosnan said as the two detectives climbed out of the car.

"Morning, Pascal. What have you got for us on this cold and frosty morning?" Flynn asked.

"It's down there," the young officer said, indicating the rocks below.

"Have you been down to have a look?" Fahy said.

"I have not! It's treacherous down there, and what good would it be if I got stuck on the rocks along with the corpse? Anyway, it stinks," Brosnan said indignantly.

"I have a rope in the car. We can tie it off around the axle, and I'll lower myself down and see what the story is," Flynn said.

Sally Fahy retrieved the bright blue nylon rope from the back of the squad car, and scrambled down on the cold grass to tie it securely around the front axle of the Hyundai. She then presented the other end of the rope to Flynn who secured it snugly under his arms and around his torso.

"Be careful, Sarge. It looks slippery down there," Fahy said.

"It'll be fine. Just make sure the handbrake is on in the car," Flynn replied walking backwards towards the precipice.

It took Eamon Flynn a good seven minutes to get down to where the remains lay between the rocks at the edge of the sea. He manoeuvred with a combination of abseiling and just scrambling against the loose stones, and relied heavily on the rope that was securing him to make the perilous journey. When he got to the bottom he managed to find a foothold on a smooth flat rock, and he bent down to examine the stinking mess. After a couple of minutes, he looked up to the two Gardaí who were peering anxiously over the edge.

"I'm coming back up. Put some tension on the rope for me," Flynn shouted, and slowly he clambered back up the near-sheer face of rock and shale, arriving back on the short grass at the top quite out of breath.

"So, what's the story?" Brosnan asked.

"Jesus, Pascal, give me a minute to get my breath back, will ye?" Flynn said, red faced and gasping slightly.

Fahy and Brosnan waited for a few moments while Flynn recovered.

"Well some bloody detective you are, Pascal. That's only a fucking sheep down there, isn't it?" Flynn said at last.

"What? You're joking me. That's no sheep, I'm telling you, it's a body!" Brosnan protested.

"I'll give you a clue, Pascal. It's a four-legged corpse, covered in rotting wool, with two pointy ears and a snout a bit like a dog. Oh, and it has a short stubby tail too. Ring any bells?" Flynn said.

"Jesus, I'm sorry, Sarge. I could have sworn it was human. And the old fella that found it said it was a body too. I just kind of assumed, if you know what I mean."

Sally Fahy had turned away from the other two, unable to keep a straight face. She could just imagine the banter in the canteen back in Galway when it came out that they had gone chasing half way across the county after a dead sheep.

9

Flynn couldn't resist rubbing it in a bit too.

"I suppose we'll have to cancel the forensic team that are on their way out too. Or would you like a post mortem carried out on the animal, so we can inform its relatives?"

"God, I'm really sorry. Will you apologise to Inspector Lyons for me?" Brosnan said.

"Oh no you don't, Pascal. You're going to call this in yourself. But do me a favour, put it on speakerphone so we can all hear her reaction. I'd say it will be priceless!" Flynn said, not intending to let the young officer off the hook that easily.

"Right. Well let's get back to the station. I'm sure you could both do with a cuppa to warm up a bit. Then I'll make the call, God help me," Brosnan said, and all three set off back to the Garda station in Roundstone.

When Pascal Brosnan had endured the ribbing on the phone from both Sergeant Mulholland and Inspector Lyons, the two Galway detectives left Roundstone and drove back to Mill Street.

"What a waste of time," Fahy said on the way back in the car.

"Ah, yeah, but it was worth it to be able to take the piss out of Brosnan for the rest of time. He'll never live this down," Flynn said.

"I hope we don't get it in the neck too," Fahy said.

"We'll be OK. It wasn't our call after all. There'll be a bit of banter about it back at the station, but we'll get over it."

Chapter Three

The following morning, Superintendent Finbarr Plunkett sat at his largely empty mahogany desk in his generously proportioned office on the third floor of the Garda station in Mill Street in Galway. Despite the inclement weather outside, typical for a December day in Galway, his office was warm, if not indeed a bit stuffy. In front of him, neatly typed on three pages of good quality cream bond paper with the gold embossed insignia of An Garda Síochána at the top of each page, was a letter from no less than the Garda Commissioner himself.

The letter was in response to a proposal Plunkett had submitted over two years previously, outlining how he wanted to expand the Detective Unit in Galway. It read:

Dear Superintendent Plunkett,
I write in connection with your proposal of February 2016 concerning the expansion of the Galway Detective Unit within the Western Region of the force. Having consulted with senior members of An

Garda Síochána, and with my colleagues who have some expertise in these matters, I am amenable to your proposal in an overall sense, but with some modifications as set out hereunder.

As you suggest, the Detective Unit should be expanded. To achieve this expansion, I propose that a new post of Detective Chief Superintendent be created, based out of the Mill Street station, and that you might consider filling this position yourself.

The vacancy at Superintendent level could therefore be filled from within your own ranks, and in keeping with your proposal, I suggest that Senior Inspector Michael Hays be made up to Detective Superintendent.

Further positions should be recruited by both Hays and yourself to bring the unit up to a new strength comprising two Detective Inspectors (one at Senior Inspector Level at your discretion), two Detective Sergeants, and three Detective Gardaí, while maintaining the current levels of civilian support and technological support for the unit.

Further assistance for the unit will be provided by additional posts in the forensic team, but these will be recruited separately through the usual channels, and you will be advised in due course.

In implementing these changes, I would ask you to have regard to the current policies on gender balance and equality within the unit, and to ensure that all of the correct procedures are followed meticulously before any appointments are made.

To allow sufficient time for the recruitment, and any additional training that may be required, these changes will take effect from June 1st next year, and budgetary adjustments will be made to reflect the new organizational structure from that time.

I will leave it to you to decide when best to share these new arrangements with your team, but please make it clear that the changes will not be effective until the date indicated, although I have no issue with any of the individuals "acting up" in the interim, provided that their pay scale remains as is until the implementation date.

As I understand it, Mill Street is currently operating above capacity, so I have today sent a note to the Office of Public Works to ask them to find a suitable overflow arrangement close to the station until such time as our new Western Regional Headquarters comes on stream in the near future.

You may contact Ms Irene McFerriter here at Headquarters for any Human Resource assistance that you may require to implement these measures.

Yours sincerely,

Dónal J. Whelan
Garda Commissioner

"Well that's a good one all right," Plunkett said to himself whilst rubbing his chin, "I thought they had forgotten all about it. It just goes to show, it always takes longer than you could imagine to accomplish anything in this outfit. Still, it's all good!"

Superintendent Plunkett lifted the phone and dialled an internal number. The phone was answered by Detective Garda Sally Fahy.

"Sally, is Inspector Hays in his office?"

"Eh yes, sir, he is."

"Could you ask him to drop up to see me if he has a few minutes? Thanks."

A few moments later, there was a knock on the superintendent's door.

"Come in, Mick. Sit you down. Coffee?" the superintendent said.

"Yes, thanks sir." Hays replied.

Plunkett rang through to his secretary and asked for two coffees, and then swivelled the letter from the Commissioner around towards Hays.

"Have a read of that, Mick. It looks as if something has come through at last."

Hays studied the letter in silence, reading through all three pages before making any comment.

"Congratulations, sir, that's excellent news. It looks as if they have agreed to just about everything you asked for," Hays said.

"I asked for a good bit more, Mick, but I've learnt in this game that's what you do – ask for a dozen, and you get three or four. It's all I really wanted anyway – we couldn't handle too much change all at once. What do you think about stepping up to Super?"

"If you're happy with it, sir, then I'd be delighted. You know it wasn't so long ago I was thinking of handing in my papers here. I had an offer to go to a UK force to head up a new digital crime unit. I'm glad I didn't now," Hays said.

"I heard about that, but I'm glad you decided to stay. So, can I assume that's a done deal then, all in due time, of course? There's a bloody lot of administration and paperwork that goes with it mind you. Less operational work. Are you OK with that?"

"Yes, sir. Perfectly, and I'm sure there will be times when I'll still be able to get my hands dirty," Hays said.

Just then the phone on the superintendent's desk rang and he picked it up.

"It's for you, Mick. You're wanted downstairs. Let's continue this discussion later, or maybe tomorrow, and in the meantime mum's the word, OK?"

"Fine, sir," Hays said getting up to leave, "and thanks."

The superintendent gave Hays a nod and went back to studying the letter.

* * *

"What's up Sally?" Hays asked Detective Garda Sally Fahy as he returned to the open plan office where the detective unit plied their trade.

"There was a call for you, sir. Some bloke called 'Rolo' or 'Rollo' he said. He said you know him. He's going to ring back in five minutes."

"Thanks Sally," Hays said and went into his private office and closed the door.

A few minutes later, his phone rang.

"Hays."

"This is Rollo. We need to meet," a man's husky voice said.

"Usual place, half an hour?" Hays said.

Rollo said nothing, and just hung up.

15

Hays collected his scarf and overcoat as he left his office and made for the door. It was December after all, and the west of Ireland weather was doing its best to dampen the Christmas spirit that seemed to have gripped the city over the past few days. The festive lights strung across the streets high up between the lamp standards were swinging wildly in the strong wind, and rain cascaded down from the gutters and parapets giving the pedestrians hurrying along beneath with parcels and shopping bags a good soaking.

Hays drove out to Salthill, where rather crude concrete shelters had been built along the promenade looking out to sea. The local youths had decorated these very basic structures with graffiti in all shapes and colours. The city council would come along in the spring and re-paint them in time for the tourist season, but for now they looked tatty and unkempt. They provided an ideal meeting place for Hays and his snout. No one would be using the shelters today, and the promenade itself was completely deserted.

Hays parked up and walked – bent against the rain – straight to the one where he met Rollo occasionally to glean information about potential criminal activity. The information Rollo gave him proved generally useful, if a little lacking in detail, but Hays used it to fill in the blanks, or to point enquiries in a particular direction, and he paid Rollo handsomely for it.

Today, he had brought a half bottle of Irish whiskey and five well used ten euro notes in the expectation that Rollo hadn't dragged him out in such awful weather for no good reason.

Hays stepped into the shelter and found Rollo already sitting inside trying to keep as far away from the driving wind and rain as it would allow. He was a man who could have been any age from forty to sixty, with lank, thinning grey hair that stuck to his scalp, a weather-beaten face that featured three or four days of grey stubble and a few badly yellowed teeth. He was wearing a heavy tweed herringbone overcoat, black trousers and badly broken cracked leather shoes that Hays assumed were nowhere near watertight. He didn't smell too good either, so Hays remained seated at the far end of the concrete bench.

"Rollo," Hays said with a nod.

"Mick," the man replied, and that was the extent of the greeting that passed between them.

"Have you got anything for me?" Rollo said.

"I hope you have something for me, Rollo, dragging me all the way out here in this weather."

"Sure, don't you know I have. I don't suppose you brought a drop of cheer considering it's so near the Christmas?" Rollo said.

Hays reached into the inside pocket of his coat and produced the half bottle of whiskey.

"Ah, God bless you, sir," Rollo said, grasping the bottle, removing the screw top and taking a generous swig.

"Ah, that's better. Fair warms the cockles, that does," Rollo said.

"C'mon Rollo, I haven't got all day. What have you got?" Hays asked.

Rollo leant in nearer to Hays giving him the full benefit of his body odour, now infused with the smell of whiskey. Hays tried not to withdraw visibly from the man.

"Just something I heard. You know the way they will be giving a double week's benefits out next week?" Rollo said.

"Yes."

"Well, seems there are a few lads fancy a bit of it, out in Clifden, I hear. They reckon there could be up to seventy or eighty grand in it – worth having a go," Rollo said.

"Who are these lads, Rollo?"

"Ah, now I don't know that, Mick. I just overheard a couple of them chatting on their phones when they were having a smoke in the back lane outside the pub. I didn't recognise them or anything."

"So, you think they're going to have a go at Clifden Post Office on benefits day next week?" Hays said.

"That's what it sounds like, Mick. Now have you anything else for me? I'm a bit brassic."

Hays slipped the notes into the man's grubby hand and they disappeared instantly.

"Ah, thanks Mick, you're a good man even if you are a copper," Rollo said.

"This better pan out, Rollo," Hays said.

"Ah 'tis sound, don't worry, sir."

Hays turned the information he had received over in his head on the way back to Mill Street.

"It sounds feasible, I suppose, if a bit daring. But that's the way things are going these days," he said to himself. By the time he got back to the station, he had almost fully bought into Rollo's story.

Chapter Four

"Where did you disappear to?" Inspector Maureen Lyons asked Hays when he returned to the office. Lyons and Hays were partners in life, as well as in the force, and they lived together in what had been Hays' house in Salthill. Lyons had moved in after being made up to inspector following the successful detection and prosecution of a particularly nasty murder a few years previously. It was an unconventional arrangement but Superintendent Plunkett tolerated it, as long as it didn't interfere with their police work, and to date it hadn't.

"I got a call from Rollo. He told me there could be a job going down out in Clifden next week on benefits day. Some likely lads reckon with the extra week it will be worth their while doing the post office. They seem to think it could be worth seventy grand," Hays said, relaying the skimpy details that Rollo had shared with him.

"Jesus, are you sure he's reliable, Mick? Clifden is the last place I'd be targeting if I was them. There's only four roads out of the place, and they basically lead nowhere anyway," Lyons said.

"I know what you mean, but there are literally hundreds of holiday homes out there, and you could be holed up in any one of them completely unobserved for days and no one would be any the wiser. Anyway, where else would you rob? Galway is a no-no due to the traffic – you'd never get out of it. Moycullen and Oughterard wouldn't be rich enough, and if you planned it right, you could be away off to Westport or back into Galway before Séan Mulholland had finished his tea and biscuits!" Hays said.

"Hmm. OK. So what day is benefits day out in Clifden anyway?" Lyons said.

"Tuesday, I think. We'll have to check up with the Department of Social Welfare to see what the drill is for getting the money out there, and how much they usually hand out in cash. I think a lot of the old-timers in the west don't have bank accounts, or even if they do, they prefer to get the readies into their hands so that they can go and play cards and have a few pints in the afternoon in front of a nice warm turf fire in some of the pubs," Hays said.

"I'll get Sally Fahy onto it straight away. If we're going to catch these buggers, we need to plan it carefully. Do you think they will be armed?" Lyons said.

"Possibly, although not heavily. Probably just a sawn-off shotgun to scare the living daylights out of the post-mistress. I doubt if they'll want to use it though," Hays said.

"Nevertheless, we'll need to get the Armed Response Unit involved just in case."

When Fahy contacted the Department of Social Welfare, she was careful not to reveal the reason for her enquiries. It was important to keep the possibility of a blag going down a secret, lest the word might get back to the gang and the entire caper be called off.

Lyons was alone in her office when Fahy knocked on her door.

"Hi Sally, what's up?" Lyons said.

"I've been onto the Department, boss. They told me that they normally send around thirty-two thousand in cash out to Clifden with the postman, who has a safe in his van. But next week, that amount will be doubled due to the Christmas bonus, so more like sixty thousand."

"Right. Well get onto the central post office here and find out what the arrangements are for the transportation of large amounts of money. Don't be specific about Clifden, and tell them we're just updating our records about cash in transit generally. Ask about Loughrea and Athenry as well in case they smell a rat," Lyons said.

* * *

Clifden post office is located on the main street, sandwiched, along with two other retail outlets, between Foyle's Hotel and Millar's knitwear and souvenir emporium. It could be a busy little place at times, and the post-mistress, Bridget O'Toole, who had run the place for more than thirty years, was frequently hard pressed to keep up without letting long queues develop. On benefits day, she often enlisted the help of her daughter, Aoife, to help out. Aoife worked in the nearby pharmacy, and took a few hours off on Tuesdays to help her mother through the busy hours from 11 a.m. to lunch time, by which time most of the benefits had been doled out.

Bridget was a small woman, with tight grey curls and a wrinkled complexion who knew absolutely everything about every single citizen from the town. Before the installation of the automated telephone exchange, which came to Clifden in the late 1980s, Bridget had manned the old manual telephone exchange in the little shop, and as a result eavesdropped on every conversation that took place between the locals, or between them and their overseas relations – usually in America.

Over the years Bridget had endured three robberies, on one occasion chasing the thieves out empty-handed with a stout hawthorn shillelagh that she kept under the counter for just such an occasion. But she was getting old now, and she knew that the thieves were getting more vicious, so recently she had adopted a different approach. These days, if an attempt was made to steal from her, she would not resist – after all, it was only money, and not even hers.

With Christmas approaching, the town was busy enough. There were no tourists of course, and all of the folks that occupied the holiday homes in the hinterland had long since departed to their busy urban lives, but nevertheless, the locals provided brisk trade in the town's shops, and for the past three weeks the post office had been busy sending parcels and packets, letters and greeting cards off to the USA, Australia, and of course all over the United Kingdom. Despite extensive advertising and postering inside the post office, people still thought they could rush in during Christmas week with a parcel for their relatives overseas, and expect it to be delivered virtually overnight. But Bridget was patient with such tardy customers, often saying, "Won't it be a nice surprise for them in the new year!" and would take the package and get it away as soon as she could.

Bridget and Aoife had worked out a practical scheme for dishing out benefits every Tuesday. Paddy McKeever would arrive out between nine thirty and ten in the morning, depending on the number of deliveries he had to make on route. On arrival, he would bring the van around to the yard at the rear of the post office, open the safe in the back of the van, and carry in the cash; then Bridget would place it all in her own safe. Then she would sign for the cash and let Paddy away before opening the packages and removing €5,000 in mixed denominations of notes and coins. She would bring this money into the front office, being careful to lock the safe again. As she handed out the allowances, giving each beneficiary the amount printed on their benefits book, Aoife would top up her supply at the front counter from the safe from time to time. It usually took about two hours to pay out to all those who wanted ready money, so that starting at eleven, they would be finished shortly after one o'clock and could go to get some lunch next door in Foyle's Hotel. It was a well-practiced routine that had served them well, and there was really nothing different about Christmas, except of course that the amount dispensed to each recipient was almost double the usual.

Chapter Five

Hays had gone upstairs to inform Superintendent Plunkett of the information he had received, and to see what additional resources he could procure to set up a stake-out in Clifden the following Tuesday.

Lyons was in her office when he re-appeared a few minutes later looking glum.

"Christ, Maureen, that man! You'd swear it was his own money," Hays said.

"That went well then. What's the story?" Lyons said.

"He will only give us two men from the Armed Response Unit. He says that you and I both have firearms authorization, and with Sally and Eamon and a couple of Séan's men in plain clothes, we should be able to handle it. But of course, if it goes wrong, it'll be my fault," Hays complained.

"Never mind, Mick, we'll be fine. Don't worry. You and I can draw guns for the day, and there'll be enough of us to deal with whatever turns up. Just try not to shoot me!"

"As if," he said, softening.

He was always surprised at just how tough his favourite Detective Inspector could be. Although she was only five foot three inches tall, and her big brown eyes and dark hair gave her a look of childing innocence, woe betide anyone who took her for a pushover. She had, after all, as a rookie uniformed Garda, arrested an armed robber making a getaway from a bank raid on Eyre Square single-handedly. On another occasion she had been taken and tied up by a nasty vicious little thug called Lorcan McFadden, but Lyons had got herself free and given McFadden a good hiding for his trouble.

"OK, well we need a good briefing on Monday. Can you get Seán to send in Jim Dolan and any others he can spare, and we'll make a plan for Tuesday? Get Sally and Eamon in too. We'll kick off at half ten – don't want to get the country folks up too early. Then see if you can set up the firearms for us both," Hays said.

"OK, will do," Lyons said, and then went on, "Mick, are you sure that Rollo's information is good? We're going to look very foolish if nothing happens."

"Not half as foolish as we will if something goes down and we failed to act on information received," he said.

"Yeah, I guess you're right."

* * *

On Friday afternoon, Superintendent Plunkett asked Mick Hays to go for a drink with him at the Golf Club out at Bearna. Although this was unusual, Hays gladly accepted. When they were seated in comfortable chairs each with a pint of Guinness in front of them in the largely deserted Golf Club members' lounge, Plunkett opened the conversation.

"Well, Mick, did you think any more about the new plans for the unit?"

"Yes, sir, I did. I think it's really good news for us. I'm happy to accept the new role, even if it does mean more emphasis on administration. I've given a bit of thought to the rest of the team too," Hays said.

"Good. What are your thoughts?" Plunkett said.

"I think Maureen would make a good senior inspector. She's got a few years under her belt as inspector now, and she handled that thing at the pony show really well. She has a lot of respect from the rest of the team too – they look to her for inspiration, and they all recognise that she's a tough cop. Would you agree?" Hays said.

"I can't disagree, Mick. Even if you may be slightly biased," Plunkett said, looking sideways at Hays with a wry smile.

"I'm trying to be objective, sir."

"And what about the rest of them?"

"I'd like to keep Eamon at sergeant for now. He's coming along, but he's not ready for inspector yet, so I'd like to bring in someone from outside for that position. That will give us the two inspectors," Hays said.

"OK, Mick, but do you not think that could be very de-motivational for him?"

"Maybe, but I'll talk to him and explain that it's not his turn just yet, but that if he continues to progress, we'll pick him up next time. Then I'd like to make Sally Fahy up to Detective Sergeant. That gives us the two we need at that level, then we can recruit three detective Gardaí from the uniformed ranks. I'll talk to Liam Dunne and he'll point a few good ones out for me."

"And this new inspector – could we take him or her from this new-fangled Graduate Entry programme they are experimenting with to keep them happy up in the Park? God, Mick, I don't know what this job is coming to at all, saints preserve us," Plunkett said.

"Well, sir, I suppose we have to move with the times. That should be fine. Expectations will be modest in any case – it might work to our advantage," Hays said.

"Good man, Mick. Will ye put all that in a memo to me next week and we'll get the thing moving before they change their minds up in Dublin. I'd hate them to think we're dragging our heels. Now, tell me, what about this thing out in Clifden?" Plunkett said.

Hays explained their plan for the following Tuesday. He had another go at getting Plunkett to agree to use more of the ARU, but Plunkett would have nothing to do with it.

"Sure you'll be grand. Yourself and Lyons will be armed, and you'll have a good few uniformed officers as well as your own team for backup. We have to be very careful about expenditure these days, as you'll soon discover, and those ARU boys charge us nearly five grand a day for their services," Plunkett said.

"I hope you're right, sir."

At that point a friend of Plunkett's came into the lounge, and Hays used the opportunity to make his excuses and depart, leaving the two men to catch up. There was only so much of Superintendent Plunkett's company he could take at a time.

Outside in the car park Hays called Lyons on his mobile phone.

"Hi. Where are you?" she said.

"I'm just leaving the Super out at the golf club. I'll be back in about twenty minutes. Are you at the station?"

"Yeah, but I'm ready to leave. I don't feel like cooking. Shall we meet somewhere?" Lyons said.

"Good idea. What do you fancy?"

"Oscar's on Dominick Street. I need a good feed of seafood, OK with you?" she said.

"Sure. Give them a call and book a table. I'll see you there in half an hour," Hays said.

"Great. See ya, bye."

* * *

When they were seated in Oscar's, their favourite seafood restaurant in the heart of the city, Hays started to outline the plans that had been approved for the unit. He explained the new positions, and emphasised that none of it would take effect for six months or more, and that she should tell no one for the moment.

"Cripes, Mick, that's great news. Congratulations to you, but listen, do you think I'll really be able to step up to your job?" Lyons said.

"Yes, I do. But seriously, it's much more important that *you* believe you can do it. It is a lot of responsibility, but I have every faith in your ability, and remember, no one gets it right every single time. And anyway, I'll still be around getting in the way."

"No, you won't. You'll be off to your budget committee meetings up in Dublin and all that palaver, and I'll be left to sort out all the shit round here. But I'm not saying I can't handle it — it'll just take a bit of getting used to, that's all."

"Do you think Eamon will be OK with staying as sergeant?" Hays asked.

"I do, to be honest. He knows he has more to do before getting inspector, I don't think it will be a problem. And Sally will be thrilled," Lyons said.

"Yes, she will, but don't breathe a word of it to her till it's all official now. And there's something else. Plunkett wants us to fill the vacant inspector's job from this new scheme the powers that be are piloting — Graduate Entry no less!"

"Bloody hell! That's all we need. Will you have to follow through on that?" she said.

"Probably. It keeps him right, and it wouldn't be a good time to piss him off."

"'Course not. I'm sure we'll survive. But listen, will you be OK giving up operational control? I figured you for a real hands-on type of cop, not a desk jockey," she said between mouthfuls of delicious pan-fried scallops.

"I don't know to be really honest, Maureen, but I think so. Anyway, I can always muscle in on some of your cases if I get bored," he said smiling.

"No chance!"

Chapter Six

It was Monday morning when the extended team assembled in the open plan office at Mill Street Garda Station. Jim Dolan had arrived in with Peadar Tobin, a uniformed officer from the Clifden station, and Detective Sally Fahy. Detective Sergeant Eamon Flynn, Garda John O'Connor, Hays and Lyons were all dotted around.

Hays outlined the information that he had been given by Rollo, and they all agreed that if a post office heist was to happen, this would be the week to do it.

Hays outlined his plan. Hays would position himself in the front lounge of Foyle's Hotel which had a bay window affording him a good view of the street and the entrance to the post office. It would only take him a few seconds to get out of the hotel to the post office if he saw anything developing. Lyons volunteered to go inside the post office and stay with Aoife and Bridget who would have to be informed of the possibility of a robbery. Flynn and Fahy would park up opposite the post office and be on standby. They would also be responsible for communications back to Galway, where John O'Connor would man the radios at this end. Dolan and Tobin were to hang around in the lane at the rear of the post office, and observe, reporting as postman Paddy McKeever arrived and keeping a sharp lookout for anything suspicious. He would leave the two ARU boys to look after themselves, as long as they were in radio contact with the rest of the team.

All of them were to be in place by nine thirty on Tuesday; they were to leave Galway city spaced ten minutes apart, from eight, so that they wouldn't draw attention to themselves. Everyone was to be in unmarked cars. Radio use was to be kept to a minimum once a radio check had been carried out when everyone was in position. The team were advised that the two senior officers would be armed, but that the intention was to preserve life as much as possible, and only to use the guns if an officer, or a member of the public, was directly threatened.

"Will Paddy McKeever be in the loop?" Flynn asked.

"No. The fewer people that know about this the better. We can't afford a leak. That would blow the entire operation," Hays said.

"But he could be in some danger, sir," Flynn persisted.

"Well, it's up to us to protect him, isn't it, Eamon. But he's not to know, my decision. Is that clear?"

"Yes, sir," Flynn said, somewhat uneasily.

* * *

The team spent the rest of the day preparing themselves for the stake out the following day. They made sure that the radios were fully charged, and at five o'clock, Mick Hays and Maureen Lyons, accompanied by Sergeant

31

Flannery made their way to the armoury in the basement where guns for the Gardaí were kept securely in locked cages.

It took them a few minutes to sign the paperwork, check the guns by cycling them a couple of times with no ammunition, and counting out the fifty Parabellum 9mm rounds allocated to each officer.

"Remember now, if you use these, collect any empty shell cases if you can, and the live rounds will have to be counted back in when it's over, and any used ones accounted for. Are you happy you can keep these in a safe place overnight?" the sergeant said.

"Yes, that's not a problem, we have a safe at home, and we'll put them both in there," Lyons said.

"Grand. Off you go then, and Inspector, good luck!" Flannery said to Hays.

As they left the station, earlier than usual for them both at five thirty, Lyons said, "I hate those damn things. I know it's good to have them just in case, but I hope we don't have to use them."

"I know what you mean. But we don't know what we're up against here – better to be well prepared," Hays said.

* * *

Tuesday morning was a dark winter's day in Galway. It didn't get bright in the area till nine o'clock at this time of year. People forget that the west of Ireland is almost forty minutes behind London in terms of the arrival of the morning light, although all of Ireland maintains Greenwich Mean Time. This results in the dawn coming later to the city, and some say, accounts for why the locals are perceived to rise later than their counterparts on the east coast of the country.

The rain was persistent, and thick heavy clouds overhead ensured that even well after sunrise, the day would remain gloomy and miserable. The weather reflected the mood of the detectives as they drove out towards Clifden with their car heaters struggling to keep the windscreens clear of mist and dampness that seemed to get into your bones.

They arrived in Clifden at roughly ten-minute intervals. Hays parked opposite the post office. It was too early for Lyons to go to the post office, so she stayed in the car while Hays crossed the road and went into Foyle's Hotel which was just waking up. He ordered coffee and toast, and took a seat in the window overlooking the street.

Fahy and Flynn arrived next, and parked a few cars down from where Lyons was waiting in Hays' car. They got out, despite the rain, and strolled slowly down Main Street browsing the shop windows at a leisurely pace. There was no one else around at all, and the two detectives tried hard not to look conspicuous in the early winter morning.

At ten past nine, Lyons saw Bridget O'Toole lift the blind on the door of the post office and turn the hanging plastic sign in the window from 'Closed' to 'Open'. She waited a few minutes more, and then got out of the car and crossed the road, entering the post office. A bell attached to the top of the door gave a loud 'ping' as the door opened, and Bridget looked up from behind the counter, surprised to have a customer so early at this time of year.

Lyons approached the counter, warrant card at the ready.

"Good morning, Mrs O'Toole," Lyons said, "my name is Inspector Maureen Lyons from the Galway Detective Unit. May we have a word please?"

"Yes, of course, inspector," Bridget said, moving towards the door at the end of the small counter. The post-mistress admitted Lyons in behind the glassed-in counter, and the two women moved around each other trying to find a comfortable position so that they could talk without being on top of one another.

"Mrs O'Toole, we have received information that there may be an attempt to carry out a robbery here this morning at your post office," Lyons said in as low key a voice as she could muster. She went on, "We have armed officers positioned out front, and two more waiting at the rear of the building for when Paddy arrives with the benefit cash."

"Oh, good God, not again. This place will be the death of me yet, I swear. And it's a double week this week too. It would be a right haul. Do you think they'll be armed?" Bridget O'Toole, who had gone several shades paler, asked, "Oh and by the way, call me Bridget – everyone does."

"We don't know, Bridget, but we're not taking any chances. What I need you to do is behave just as you usually do. If it's OK with you, I'll stay out front here with you, acting as your assistant for the day," Lyons said.

"What about Aoife? She usually helps out on benefits day."

"That's fine. Tell her if you like, but let's keep her out the back. She'll be safer there if anything goes off. What time does Paddy usually arrive with the cash?" Lyons said.

"Depends on the traffic in the city, but he's nearly always here by about ten past ten. I don't even have time to give the poor man a cuppa tea after his long drive like I do every other day. It's all go once the cash is here. They start coming in at round ten minutes to eleven, even though we don't start handing it out till the top of the hour. Then it's non-stop till dinner hour," Bridget said.

* * *

Paddy McKeever arrived into the depot at his usual time of 6:30 a.m. Given the time of year, even at this early hour, the place was a hive of activity. A large green pantechnicon was parked in the yard, with forklift trucks darting to and fro unloading pallets of parcels and sacks of mail, and taking them indoors to be sorted and sent back out for delivery. The truck had driven up from Shannon where it had been filled with items that had arrived in from the USA by freight plane earlier in the night.

Paddy's bags were ready for him, and he loaded them into his van in the correct order, so that he would have the right one to hand when he reached Moycullen and Oughterard. Parcels filled the back part of his vehicle, mostly wrapped in brown paper and tied with string, with large flowing handwriting to direct the goods to the sender's relatives to let them know that although they were far away, they were not forgotten.

With the van sitting low on its springs, Paddy made his way to the cash office where he withdrew the Social Welfare money bound for Clifden and signed all the required paperwork. He then took the package of notes and coins directly to the van, observing that it was significantly heavier than usual, and locked it into the safe that had been fitted inside the side door of the vehicle, putting the keys carefully into his coat pocket.

He left the depot again soon after seven, and made his way to the N59 that would take him out through Moycullen, Oughterard, Maam Cross, Recess, then into Roundstone and finally on out to Clifden where he would arrive at around ten o'clock. He was thankful that although the day was dark and wet, the temperature was well above freezing, and although it was Christmas week, he would have the road largely to himself for the journey so early in the morning.

Chapter Seven

By ten o'clock everyone was in place. The two local Gardaí were positioned outside the post office yard in plain clothes. To make it look authentic, they had the bonnet of a car raised, and were poking around in the engine compartment.

Hays was on his third cup of coffee in the hotel keeping a sharp eye out on the street. Fahy and Flynn were still window shopping, but it looked more realistic now. The street had become busier as the rain had eased off, and the sky was brighter, if only a little.

Lyons was trying to keep out of Bridget O'Toole's way as she busied herself in the little office getting ready for the onslaught. Lyons fingered her gun every few minutes which was clipped into a holster on her belt with her civilian jacket just about concealing it, and all the other paraphernalia she was carrying to defend herself if things got rough.

By twenty past ten, Bridget was getting extremely restless.

"God, I hope he comes soon. We have to unbag the cash and make up stacks of fifties, twenties and tens below the counter, not to mention the coins, before things get too busy, or we'll never get done," she said.

Just as she was about to offer the woman some soothing words, Hays came hurrying into the shop. He was half-way in when he said, "Maureen, I need a word, now!"

Lyons let herself back out into the shop through the door at the end of the counter.

"What's up?"

"Outside," he said, nodding towards the door.

When they were both outside, Hays started talking quickly.

"Mulholland has just been on the phone. He's had a call from Pascal Brosnan out in Roundstone. The postman's van has been ambushed, and the driver is dead. The money is gone."

"Jesus Mick! What do you want me to do?"

"I'm going up there now. Will you stay here for a few minutes? Get Sally to stay with the post office woman. They'll need to organise more cash or there will be a riot. Get Eamon to stay here too till things become a little clearer. When you have that set up, follow me in to Roundstone. The ambush was on the road just this side of the village. I'll get the doctor and forensics out," Hays said.

Lyons went back into the post office, and when Bridget opened the door, she re-entered the area behind the counter.

"Is there somewhere we could sit down, Bridget?" Lyons said.

"What's wrong girl?" the woman said. "You've gone fierce pale."

"I have some bad news, Bridget – very bad news."

Lyons went on to tell Bridget O'Toole about the attack on the post office van, and that the driver appeared to have been badly wounded or maybe even killed in the ambush.

"Good God, the poor man. I hope he will be all right. He has a wife and two daughters you know," Bridget said.

"Well Inspector Hays is on his way there now, and we'll know more in a while. But listen, won't you need to get another delivery of cash out here or you'll have a hundred angry pensioners on your hands?" Lyons said.

"I suppose so," Bridget said with little enthusiasm.

"Give me the number that you call in Galway and I'll arrange it for you. Could you make us all a cup of tea, Bridget?"

"Yes, yes, I'll get the number for you now. Thanks inspector."

Lyons telephoned the number Bridget had given her and got through to the main post office in Galway. After a few false starts, she finally established contact with the cash office and explained the situation to the manager there.

"You'll need to get another delivery out to Mrs O'Toole in Clifden as soon as possible. The pensioners are starting to arrive to collect their double week. I've put a notice on the door saying that benefits won't be available till two thirty for technical reasons, but we won't be able to hold them back much beyond that. If you get it ready, I'll arrange an armed escort for the delivery van. They'll be with you in half an hour or so. And if you have any

39

information of the serial numbers of the notes that were stolen, could you call it through to Garda John O'Connor at Mill Street?" Lyons said.

"Yes of course. There were a lot of new notes in the van. The Central Bank increase the money supply at this time of year, and they push the extra out through the post office system, as well as through the banks. We should be able to identify which notes went out to Clifden. And tell me, is Paddy McKeever OK?" the manager asked.

"We'll know more when the team get to where the ambush took place. Right now all we know is that it was an armed raid, and we think there was violence involved," she said, not wanting to pass on the bad news till it had been confirmed.

Next Lyons rang John O'Connor in Mill Street and asked him to arrange for more ARUs to accompany the second delivery of benefits money to Clifden, and to liaise with the cash manager at the main post office to set it up. She requested that the ARU remain in Clifden outside the post office, front and back, till it closed at five o'clock. She also told O'Connor that the man should be calling through with information about the serial numbers of the stolen notes, and that he should get the list out to all the banks in the area as soon as possible.

Then Lyons sat down with Bridget O'Toole and her daughter in the back of the post office and had a cup of tea. The post mistress was visibly shaken by the events that had taken place, so Lyons tried to get her to focus on the main business of the day.

"I've arranged for another delivery of cash for you, Bridget. It should be here at around half past one or two o'clock. It's coming with an armed guard, and they'll stay here until all the money has been handed out just in case there are any more shenanigans. I have to go now, but Detective Fahy and Detective Flynn will stay around here, and you have the two uniformed Gardaí out the back too, so you should be OK," Lyons said.

* * *

Hays pushed his Mercedes as fast as he dared along the old bog road between Clifden and Roundstone. He sped through Ballyconneely, and on past Murvey and Callow before arriving at the scene of the heist just before Dog's Bay.

Brosnan, who ran the little Garda station on the edge of Roundstone village single-handedly, had put up blue and white tape all around the small green and white An Post van that stood forlornly at the side of the road. The windscreen had been blown out, and blood and brain tissue were spread all over the panel behind where the driver would have been sitting. Paddy McKeever's body was still in the van, slumped across the two front seats. The side door of the van was open, and through it the open safe could be seen with its door hanging open, and the contents clearly missing.

The rain was holding off for the moment, but it wasn't far away. Heavy dark grey clouds hung low over the scene, adding to the grimness, and the top of Errisbeg was shrouded in a thick mist.

"Good morning, Inspector," Brosnan said, walking over to Hays' car as the senior man got out.

"Morning, Pascal. This is a rum do. I presume the poor man is dead?"

"He sure is, sir. Not much of him left above the neck to be honest. They must have fired through the windscreen and the pellets got mixed with glass splinters to do that much damage to a man," Brosnan said.

"Bastards! Right. I have the doctor and the forensic team on the way out. How long ago did it happen do you know?"

"I can't be exactly sure, sir. But I heard the shot at about half past nine. There's no shooting in these parts at this time of year, so I came out to investigate, and found poor Paddy here myself," the Garda said, clearly shaken by the discovery.

"Have you done anything about sealing off the area?"

"Well, I called Sergeant Mulholland, and he sent a car out towards Recess to set up a check point, but with some of his men staked out at the post office, that's the best he could do. Galway have a couple of cars on the way out, but the buggers could be well away by now, out towards Letterfrack, or even on into Clifden and away towards Westport," Brosnan said.

"Right. Well get onto Westport and get them to join in the search as well. They can put a checkpoint up and make sure the instruction is stop and search all vehicles – no exceptions."

"Yes, sir. Right away, sir."

Hays put blue overshoes on his feet and ducked under the tape. He walked all around the van, looking carefully at the ground. He noticed that the key was still dangling from the lock of the safe inside.

He then expanded his circle around the van, and examined the grass at the side of the road where the vehicle had come to rest. He spotted a spent shotgun cartridge in the long grass, and went and got a yellow plastic marker with the number 2 on it, and placed it alongside the item without disturbing it.

Pascal Brosnan was busy stopping the few cars that arrived at the scene and turning them back the way they had come.

Hays' phone rang. It was Maureen Lyons calling from her car.

"Hi. What's the story?" she said.

"It's pretty bad, Maureen. Paddy McKeever has had his head blown off with a shotgun. The cash is all gone, and Pascal wasn't able to arrange road blocks quickly enough to apprehend them. But they may not have gone very far anyway," Hays said.

"How do you mean?"

"Well, think about it. If I was them, I'd probably hole up in one of the many empty holiday homes round here somewhere for a few days rather than risk getting caught on the road. What do you think?"

"You could well be right. Needle in a haystack then. Listen, we better get someone out to Mrs McKeever before the rumour mill gets to her first. Can you call the station and get two uniforms out to the house?" Lyons said.

"Yeah, I'll call it in now. One of each, I guess?"

"What?" she said.

"One male and one female Garda – would you agree?"

"Oh, yes, of course. Thanks. See you in about ten minutes," Lyons said.

As Lyons approached the scene of the crime, there was a short queue of eight cars backed up behind Pascal Brosnan's roadblock. It was taking all of his persuasive

43

powers to convince the locals that they needed to go back out the road and endure a twelve-mile detour over narrow boggy boreens to get what was normally less than a mile into the village.

Lyons put on the siren in her Ford Focus and drove down the wrong side of the road till she arrived at the Garda tape.

She got out and joined her partner at the side of the road.

"Christ, Mick, this is a mess. Poor old guy. Don't worry, we'll get the toe-rags that did this. If it were up to me, I'd hang them!" Lyons said.

Chapter Eight

It seemed ages before the sirens belonging to Sinéad Loughran's Toyota Landcruiser penetrated the stillness. She pulled the vehicle to a halt on the Roundstone side of the cordon, and alighted briskly from the vehicle. Dr Julian Dodd, the pathologist attached to the force, took a little longer to climb down from the passenger's seat of the jeep. He was quite a short man, which may, in part, have accounted for his slightly pompous demeanour. But the detectives were happy to overlook this foible – he was a damn fine doctor, and had helped them to solve some very tricky cases over the past several years. As always he was dapper, dressed in a charcoal grey suit and pale blue shirt with a silk tie carefully knotted at the collar.

"Hello Sinéad, Doctor," Lyons said as the two approached. Loughran had already donned her white scene of crime suit, overshoes, and bright blue gloves, and was ready to get to work on the scene at once, realising that time was of the essence.

"Hi Maureen," Loughran said, "I'll do the outside till the Doc has finished with the driver, if that's OK?"

"Yes please, Sinéad, Mick has already found a spent cartridge over there in the grass. He has it marked."

Hays watched Julian Dodd examine the body of Paddy McKeever in the front of the post office van. After a few moments, the doctor straightened up and reversed out of the front of the cab and stood on the road.

"What can you tell us, Doc?" Hays asked.

"Well apart from the blindingly obvious, not much. He died instantly from shotgun pellets and glass that entered the frontal lobe of his brain and severed the carotid artery for good measure. I'd say the gunman was standing almost directly in front of the vehicle when he let rip. The van was stopped. Time of death, around nine thirty, give or take. Not much else I can add really. I'll write it up and send it on. I doubt there's to be a post mortem unless you want to know what he had for breakfast," the doctor quipped.

"It's OK, Doc, that won't be necessary. Can you wait for Sinéad to finish up for a lift back to town?" Hays said.

"I'll stroll into the village and get a cup of coffee in the Bogbean Café opposite Eldon's Hotel. Ask her to stop by and collect me when she's done, would you?"

"Yes, sure. Thanks," Hays said.

Sinéad Loughran and her two assistants spent the next hour and a half combing out the area all around the scene and fingerprinting the van all over, taking special care with the door jambs and the safe.

"Anything?" Lyons asked her when she appeared to have finished.

46

"Not much, Maureen. They were obviously gloved up. There's a small blood stain on the door of the safe. Could be the driver's, but just now I'm not sure how that would have been transferred. Can we get the van lifted back to Galway? I can do some more work on it there," Loughran said.

"Yes, sure. I'll get Pascal Brosnan to arrange it. Let me know if you find anything," Lyons said.

When Lyons had spoken to Pascal Brosnan, he called Tadgh Deasy. Deasy ran a garage of sorts out the far side of Roundstone village. He repaired cars, vans and tractors, and occasionally traded one or two mostly very old cars and commercial vehicles too. He had a tow truck with a large flat bed at the back, and the Gardaí had used his services previously to move vehicles around after they had become immobile following accidents and the like. The Gardaí suspected that some of Deasy's dealings were a bit iffy, but it suited them to leave well alone, unless he became involved in anything serious.

Deasy arrived with the tow truck twenty minutes later and hoisted the broken van onto the back of it, and set off, with instructions to transport it to the locked compound at the rear of the main Garda station in Mill Street.

With the vehicles removed, one of Sinéad's team swept the broken glass and debris off the road, and finally, Pascal Brosnan was able to remove the tape that he had used to close off the road, and allow the traffic to flow freely again.

"Let's see if O'Dowds is serving lunch," Lyons said to Hays, "I'm starving."

* * *

When Hays and Lyons were seated in O'Dowds in front of a warming turf fire, with bowls of rich seafood chowder in front of them, Hays began the conversation.

"What do you make of it?" he asked Lyons.

"It's a bit of a cock-up, Mick. Rollo's information was only half right, and it makes us look pretty ham-fisted to be honest. It won't take long for the word to get around that we've made a mess of it. Have you told Plunkett?" she said.

"No, not yet. That's not a job you can tackle on an empty stomach!"

They finished their soup in silence, and waited till the server had taken away the bowls and replaced them with a generous plate of lamb shank with carrots and mashed potato.

"Mmm. This looks good. Just what we need for a day like today," Lyons said.

And they went on to eat their meal. Even though they said nothing, their brains were working at full tilt, each wondering how they could capture the perpetrators of the deadly deed and save some remnants of their reputation.

"OK," Lyons said, sitting back on the bench when she had finished eating. "Let's take stock. Do you think they've got clean away?"

"Possibly. But let's think. If you were planning this robbery, you wouldn't be sure that you could get clear before checkpoints were set up. So, if I were them, I'd definitely have a plan B," Hays said.

"And that would be?"

"I'd have a bolt hole lined up. Somewhere well out of the way with provisions, where I could stay for a good few days till things quietened down, and then use the lull over Christmas Day to get clear."

"Do you think they meant to shoot the driver?" Lyons said.

"I doubt if there was any need to. Paddy was hardly a threat after all. So, they must be vicious bastards, unless he drove at them. The doctor said the gun was fired from just in front of his van."

"Let's get back into town and see if John or Sinéad have dug up anything for us," Lyons said. "I'll drive, and you can call the Super on the way," Lyons said.

"Thanks a bunch!"

* * *

On the way back to the city, the rain had started in earnest again, adding to their already glum frame of mind. They passed the roadblock that had been set up on the road into Recess, stopping just long enough to establish that there was nothing of interest to report.

When they got past it, Hays called Superintendent Plunkett and gave him an update on the situation. Plunkett wasn't happy, and told Hays that they needed to get the mess sorted out quickly. He asked to be updated as soon as there were any developments.

They arrived back into Mill Street shortly before three o'clock.

As they walked towards their respective offices, Lyons said, "I'll get on to Sinéad and see if she's got started on the van. We might get lucky."

"Hmph," grunted Hays in reply. He wasn't feeling very lucky.

"Right. Let's have a briefing in an hour, I'll get everyone in," Lyons said.

Lyons called Sinéad Loughran on her mobile phone.

Sinéad Loughran was the team leader of the forensic crew that worked with the detectives and uniformed Gardaí in Galway. She had a staff of five, including four more forensic technicians and an administrator. Sinéad was well liked in the force. Despite her often grim work, she managed to keep a cheerful disposition, and Maureen Lyons and herself quite often went out for a few drinks after work to give out about the men in their lives and how the job was becoming almost impossible these days. Sinéad was a pretty blonde girl who usually wore her shoulder length hair in a ponytail. She was nearly always seen in a white all over forensic paper suit, which totally disguised her neat size eight figure.

"Hi, Sinéad. Just wondering if you've got anything? We're a bit desperate here," Lyons said.

"Tell me about it. We're working on the van now. They were obviously gloved up, and there aren't even any shoe or boot prints in the back. I did manage to lift a partial thumb print off the key to the safe, but it's not enough to generate a match I'm afraid. We'll keep going and hope we get lucky," Sinéad said.

"OK. Thanks. Any clue as to how many of them there was?"

"No, 'fraid not. They were either very clever or very lucky. Look, I'd best get on. I'll call you later."

"OK. Talk soon."

* * *

At four o'clock, Hays headed up the briefing meeting. Lyons had set up a board in the open plan, and on it there was a photo of the scene, a blow up of Paddy McKeever taken from his An Post security pass, and the figure

50

€64,580, which was the amount that the cashier at the main post office had said was in the van's safe.

"OK. What have we got, John?"

John O'Connor was a young uniformed Garda attached to the unit. His core competence was that he was a technical geek, and could extract an enormous amount of information from a mobile phone or a computer, not to mention his ability to discover almost everything about anyone from the internet.

"I spoke to the cashier at the cash office in Galway. He told me that at this time of year, most of the notes they handle are new notes issued by the central bank to top up the money supply for Christmas. After a bit of checking around, he was able to identify the particular batch of notes that went to Clifden, and he gave me the serial numbers. I've circulated all the banks in the area who said they would watch out for them. The bank in Clifden were particularly helpful," O'Connor said.

"What do you think the chances are?" Lyons said.

"Pretty good, I'd say. The only thing is that they may get a bit overwhelmed with new notes. The second delivery of cash was much the same as the first one," O'Connor said.

"Thanks John. Maureen, did Sinéad get anything?" Hays said.

"Not yet. She got a partial print from the key to the safe, but not enough for a match. But she's not finished yet. She's going to call me later."

"Right, well let's hope for something there. Is there any news from the checkpoints?"

"Nothing, boss," Sally Fahy said. "Do you want them manned through the night?"

"What do you think, Maureen?" Hays said.

"I don't think so. I don't think we're going to nab these guys on the road. They're too clever for that. Stand them down at seven o'clock," Lyons said.

Then Hays went on, "Now, I want everyone out among the low-life of Galway for the next couple of days. I'll talk to Rollo again and see if he can remember anything else, or he might have heard something since. You folks milk any contacts you have: snouts, small time thieves. I'm going to see if I can get Plunkett to spring for a reward – you know – for information leading to the arrest and prosecution. I'm going to ask him for €10,000, so that might loosen a few tongues."

A murmur went around the room. It wasn't often that the Gardaí put up a reward for information, but this was an exceptional situation. Hays hoped that the sympathy felt towards the murdered postman together with the incentive offered might bring some useful information to the fore.

Chapter Nine

Despite the best efforts of the Galway detectives, by the following Monday, they were no further on with the case. The €10,000 reward had been agreed, and all the local newspapers had carried headlines shouting about the callous murder of a popular man as he went about his daily toil. For the detectives, this was a double-edged sword. On the one hand, the coverage could help them to uncover information about the crime, but as time went on, a certain amount of anger turned in their direction because no visible progress was being made.

Superintendent Plunkett was getting very restless too. He was torn between letting Hays and co. get on with it — they had a very good track record after all — or calling in a team from Dublin to take over the investigation. He didn't want to do that, but the negative publicity about his unit was beginning to unsettle the powers that be in the Phoenix Park, and he was conscious that failure at this point could jeopardise his master plan for the unit.

Hays and Lyons were in Hays' office going back over the few meagre facts that they had come up with since the robbery when John O'Connor knocked on the door.

"Excuse me boss, I've just had a call from the bank in Clifden. They've taken in a bunch of those fifties that were stolen from the post office van."

"Great. How much?" Lyons asked.

"Fifteen hundred. Consecutive serial numbers," O'Connor said.

"Do they know where they came from?" Lyons said.

"That's the good bit. They were in a lodgement made by Tadgh Deasy this morning."

"Were they now! OK, John, that's great. Thanks. We'll get onto it right away," Hays said.

"Let's go!" Hays said to Lyons when O'Connor had left the room. "We can call Brosnan on the way out and get him to meet us at Deasy's."

* * *

The weather was still dark and gloomy as they drove out through Moycullen, Oughterard, Maam Cross and Recess on their way to Roundstone. The rain was holding off, but the thick grey clouds and poor light gave the usually colourful scenery a monochrome appearance, as if they were driving through a black and white photograph.

They pulled into Deasy's yard; Hays' Mercedes sliding to a halt on the greasy surface. Pascal Brosnan had already arrived and was leaning up against his own car chatting to Tadgh.

As they got out of the car, Deasy came across towards them.

"Good morning, Inspectors. Is there something I can do for you?"

"Good morning, Mr Deasy. Is there somewhere we can talk? Inside perhaps?" Lyons said.

"Here will do fine. What's on your mind?" Deasy said.

Hays engaged with the man as Lyons split away from them and went snooping around the yard.

"All right, Mr Deasy, but before we start I'm going to have to caution you." Hays went on to issue the standard caution.

Deasy looked a bit surprised but said nothing other than to confirm that he understood.

"I believe you made a lodgement in the bank in Clifden earlier today, is that correct?"

"Yes, that's right," Deasy confirmed.

"How much did you lodge?" Hays said.

"One thousand five hundred euro in cash and two cheques, one for eighty euro and the other was for one hundred and sixty euro."

"And where did you get the cash from, Mr Deasy?"

"Well, I do buy and sell a few yokes now and then. I sold a jeep to two lads here last week, and they paid me in cash."

"Did they just walk in?" Hays said.

"No, no. They brought in an old pale blue Ford Mondeo. It might have been one of yours. It had holes in the bodywork where you lot put your aerials and stuff. I gave them a hundred and fifty for it against the jeep. It was in a bad state."

"And where is the car now?" Hays said looking around to see if he could see it.

"Well that's the funny thing. They gave me an extra hundred if I promised to take the car to the crusher, so I did."

"For fuck sake, Tadgh. Where did you take it?"

"That place down by the docks in Galway. They scrap anything. Then it gets shipped out to Germany where it's all melted down to make new BMWs," Deasy said with a wry grin.

"Stay there," Hays said, turning away and calling the station.

He got through to Sally Fahy very quickly and told her to take Eamon with her and get down to the scrap yard at the docks and see if they still had the old Mondeo. If they had, she was to secure it and get it taken back to Mill Street.

"Mr Deasy, I have to inform you that the money that you lodged in Clifden today came from the proceeds of a robbery in which a man was murdered. So, I'm afraid we'll have to take you in for questioning. For now, I'll not arrest you, provided you come quietly."

"Jesus, Mick, I never had nothing to do with that. Sure, wasn't I the one who came out and took the van away? You can't think I'd be involved in any of that stuff," Deasy protested.

"Well, let's see, but for now, I want you to go with Pascal to Roundstone Garda station, and we'll be along in a few minutes. As far as anyone is concerned, you're helping the Gardaí with enquiries."

* * *

Sally Fahy used the blue lights and sirens on her Hyundai i40 to get down to the scrapyard as quickly as she could. The two detectives screamed into the yard where cars were piled one on top of another to a height of ten metres in several stacks. All around, piles of crunched up metal stood waiting for the next part of their journey, and in the very middle of the yard a huge crane with a large round magnet dangling from its steel ropes swung from side to side. High up in the cab, an old man with thin grey hair and a large beer belly, with what had once been a high visibility jacket, but was now an unpleasant shade of grey, sat at the controls.

Dangling from the magnet, a pale blue Ford Mondeo swung wildly about as the operator edged the crane towards a huge car crusher.

Fahy leapt out of the car and ran across to the crane holding up her warrant card. She made sideways movements with her hand left and right across her throat in the universal signal to kill the machine. The operator behaved lazily, but gradually the din of the crane's engine faded, and the black smoke that had been belching from its exhaust petered out. The man climbed down awkwardly from the cab, and stood beside his behemoth of a machine.

"Thank you, sir. My name is Detective Garda Fahy, and this is my colleague, Detective Sergeant Flynn. May I ask when that car came in?" Fahy said pointing to the Mondeo dangling precariously from the crane.

"Friday," the man, clearly not much of a conversationalist, said gruffly.

"We believe that vehicle may have been involved in a crime. I wonder if you could release it from the crane for us. We need to impound it."

The man said nothing, but turned his back on the two detectives, and climbed laboriously up the metal steps of the crane back into the cab. The machine wheezed and coughed before the engine roared back to life.

The Mondeo swung crazily towards them, and descended towards the dirty yard. When it was about six feet off the ground, the man released the magnet, and the car crashed to earth with a noisy thud, the jolt causing the boot to fly open and a door mirror to detach and roll on the ground.

Flynn looked up at the man with a scowl. He made a twisting motion with his hand, indicating that he was looking for the key. The man signalled from the cab of the crane to a large metal bin over beside the shed that served as a very scruffy office. Flynn walked over to find the bin more than half full with what must have been several hundred car keys.

"This is hopeless, Sally. We'll never find the right one, and that's assuming it will still be driving. But we can't leave here without it — anything could happen. Let's improvise."

The two detectives scouted round the yard till they found a stout piece of rope that was about five metres long. Flynn used an old sack on the ground to protect his clothes, and bent down, tying the rope around the front axle of the old Mondeo. He tied the other end to the towing eye of the Hyundai.

"You're in the Mondeo," he said to Fahy.

"Oh, thanks a lot. And I don't want to hear a word about women drivers. Go slowly now, won't you?" Fahy said.

They made a peculiar little convoy driving the two kilometres back to Mill Street. Flynn in front with the blue lights flashing, and the old beaten up Mondeo crabbing along at the end of the tow rope. It took them just ten minutes to make the journey, and they were glad to get the vehicle back into the secure yard at the rear of the station.

Once they were back inside the station, Flynn called Sinéad Loughran.

"Hi Sinéad. It's Eamon Flynn. We've brought in a blue Mondeo that we think may have been used for the heist out at Roundstone where the postman got shot. Could you come down with a couple of your guys and give it a good going over for us? It's in the yard at the back."

"Sure Eamon, we'll be down in a few minutes, and let's hope we get something from it. I hope there isn't a dead sheep in the boot!" Sinéad said.

"Ha ha – very funny! They obviously thought it would be crushed by now, so they may not have been too careful about it. Anyway, we'll see. Thanks."

Then Flynn called Lyons and told her that they had managed to rescue the Mondeo from the jaws of the crusher, and had it back at the station with forensics ready to start work on the car.

"Great, well done you two," Lyons said.

Chapter Ten

Tadgh Deasy sat very uncomfortably in the little place that had been set up as a makeshift interview room in the small new Garda Station at the edge of Roundstone village. Hays had shown him in there, and told him to stay put while he went to get two cups of coffee and a notepad.

"Look, Inspector, this is nuts. You people know me. I wouldn't get involved in anything like that," Deasy said as Hays re-entered the room and placed the drinks on the table.

"A man has been murdered, Mr Deasy. There are procedures that need to be followed. And you were, of your own admission, in possession of money from the proceeds of an armed robbery. So, if you've any sense, you'll answer my questions honestly," Hays said.

Deasy wriggled a bit in his seat and reached for his coffee without saying a word.

"Now, who were these two boyos that traded the Mondeo for a jeep on Friday? I need names, addresses," Hays demanded.

"I dunno, do I? They just came in like, and I've had that old jeep for ages. I was delighted to be getting rid of the thing, and they gave me good money for it. It wasn't worth much."

"Names?"

Deasy shook his head, looking at the floor.

"Well what did they look like? You must remember that at least," Hays said, losing his patience.

"Just average blokes. The younger one had a woolly hat, and the older one was very scruffy with dirty fair hair," Deasy said.

"God give me strength! You do realise it's an offence not to complete an RF105 form when you sell a vehicle, Mr Deasy, don't you?"

"Ah, look, things don't always get done like that out here in the country, specially with a couple of old jalopies," Deasy said.

"The age of the vehicle is not the issue here. Now, what was the make, model and reg. number of the jeep?" Hays asked.

"It was a Mitsubishi Pajero, green it was, and it was 98G something or other."

"I'll need the full number, and I need it now," Hays said. He was getting very fed up with Deasy's attitude.

"Let me ring Shay, he'll have it. He always remembers them things."

Hays nodded, signalling that the man could use his mobile phone to make the call. Shay, Deasy's son, did indeed remember the number of the Pajero, and Deasy relayed it to Hays, who wrote it on his pad. He then called Pascal Brosnan in from the outer office, and gave him the vehicle description, asking him to circulate it as soon as possible, and to be certain to add "approach with caution – occupants may be armed" to the bulletin.

Hays continued the questioning when Brosnan had left to put the word out on the old jeep.

"Why did you take the vehicle into Galway to the scrap yard?" he asked.

"They gave me an extra €100 for that, so I wasn't going to complain, was I?" Deasy said.

"But surely you must have been suspicious about it. Why didn't you report it?"

"Look, Inspector, you've seen my place, I'm not living the high life now, am I? Money is hard to come by doing what I'm doing, so when a couple of guys come in and offer me over the odds for an old heap, and then sweeten the deal with a few extras, I'm hardly going to turn it down, now am I?"

"And when they peeled off a pile of crisp new fifty-euro notes, you still didn't think that there was anything fishy? C'mon, Mr Deasy, you're not an idiot, now are you?" Hays said.

"I was concentrating on getting as much as I could for the Pajero. I wasn't focussed on the money till the deal was struck. To be honest, the whole thing did smell a bit off, but who was I to look a gift horse in the mouth?" Deasy said.

Hays had some sympathy for the man. He knew that Deasy's operation was marginal at best, and he could easily see how the transaction with the Mondeo and the jeep could have seemed almost too good to be true for him. And he didn't really believe that Deasy was directly involved with the robbery, but he wasn't going to let his prey off the hook too easily.

"Well, we'll be confiscating the cash — it's obviously the proceeds of a crime. The bank will debit your account. And I want you to think very carefully, Mr Deasy. If you know anything, anything at all, about who these two clients are, or where they might be staying, you need to come forward with that information urgently. If I find out later that you knew them, even vaguely, and you've held anything back, then I promise you, it will go very badly for you. Is that clear?" Hays said.

"Yes, yes of course, but I promise you, I never seen them before. But if they come back, I'll let you know, promise."

"Right. That's all for now. Off you go, and consider yourself lucky that I didn't charge you," Hays said.

When Deasy had left the station, Lyons told Hays about the recovery of the old blue Mondeo from the scrapyard.

"Well that's something at least. Has Sinéad got hold of it yet?" Hays said.

"Yes. She's working on it now," Lyons said.

"Good. Let's get back to town before dark. Maybe Sinéad will have something for us."

* * *

They arrived back in Mill Street and brought the team together for an update. Hays outlined the interview that they had had with Tadgh Deasy.

"Do you think he's involved?" Eamon Flynn asked when he heard the story of how the stolen notes had turned up in Deasy's lodgement.

"I doubt it, at least not in the robbery, but it was dumb of him not to report what was obviously a seriously suspicious transaction. Let's keep an eye on him for a while, see if anything else comes to light. I've asked Pascal Brosnan to keep us posted," Hays said.

Hays looked at Lyons indicating that she should take over.

"Sally, will you give Sinéad a call and see if she's got anything from the Mondeo?" Lyons said.

"Right, boss."

"Eamon, I want you to call Pascal and Séan and see if there's been any sightings out west. Maybe one of the checkpoints has turned up something. And if anyone has anything, bring it to me immediately, don't wait till our next meeting. It's imperative we apprehend this lot quickly or we'll be slaughtered in the media," Lyons said.

When they had dispersed, Hays and Lyons went to his office.

"Any thoughts?" Lyons said.

"It's a bit odd, don't you think? They appear to have gone to ground somewhere in the Roundstone area, but why haven't they hightailed it out of there?" Hays said.

Sally Fahy knocked at Hays' door.

"Come in, Sally. What have you got?" Lyons said.

"Sinéad found some interesting stuff in the Mondeo, Inspector. They must have thought that Deasy would have it crushed long before we got to it. As well as a reasonable crop of fingerprints, she found a plastic wrapper on the floor that came from a €5,000 bundle. It has distinct prints on it, and branding from the bank and the post office."

"Nice one, Sally. Have you run the prints yet?" Hays said.

"Yes, sir. They belong to an Anselm Geraghty, he's well known to us. In fact, he's just finished a five year stretch for aggravated burglary and actual bodily harm.

Apparently, he beat up the owner of a petrol station quite unnecessarily during a robbery when the man was closing up for the night. He was caught on CCTV, as was his brother, Emmet. It seems they often work together," Fahy said.

"Nice. OK, well get a bulletin out to all stations – you know the usual, 'approach with caution – may be armed', and see if you can get it into the local papers for tomorrow too. I take it we have some reasonably good mug shots?" Hays said.

"Yes, sir, that's no problem," Fahy said.

"Oh, and there's one more thing, sir. The younger brother's prints were found on the spent shot gun cartridge we recovered from the scene too, so it looks like it's the two of them again."

When Sally Fahy had left the office to attend to the notices, Lyons asked Hays, "What do we do now?"

"Let's see where these two bozos hail from. Where's their family home. Then we can get the local Gardaí to keep an eye out for them in case they have a strong homing instinct. Can you do that? Give them the details of the Pajero too. I'm going to update Plunkett," Hays said.

* * *

On the way home in the car, Lyons said to Hays, "How did you get on with Plunkett? You didn't say."

"He's pretty up tight. He thinks if we don't get a quick result on this that Dublin will insist on taking it over, and that could affect his master plan quite badly. But apart from that, he was pretty supportive, though of course he wasn't best pleased that we had half the force staked out in Clifden at enormous expense when the blag was going off somewhere else. Those Armed Response guys really know how to charge for their services. I know it's only 'funny money', but that little caper cost the boss €18,000 straight out of his already depleted budget. He said he'd have to push it into next year."

"That'll be you next year, you know. All spreadsheets and reports, budgets and resource management. You won't have a minute for us poor coppers out lifting thieves and murderers, wait till you see," Lyons said.

"You'll be grand without me getting in your way, Maureen. Give you a chance to shine even more than you have already."

Lyons said nothing.

Chapter Eleven

They had been in the station for about an hour, and were sitting in Hays' office reading the overnight activity logs together, when the phone on Hays' desk sprang to life.

"Inspector Hays? It's Séan Mulholland here from Clifden."

"Good morning, Séan. How's things?"

"I've just had the manager of the bank here in Clifden on to me. He's been opening the night safe bags, and he's found a couple more of those €50 notes in the lodgement from O'Dowds out in Roundstone," Mulholland said.

"I see. Did you tell him to put them away somewhere safe for us?"

"Sure, of course I did. He's got them set aside in a plastic bag, and he says he'd debited the O'Dowd account with the €100 too."

"Always the banker, eh? Right, listen I'll come out directly with Inspector Lyons. Could you get one of your lads to meet us at O'Dowds?" Hays said.

"Right, no bother. I'll get Jim Dolan on it in about half an hour. That'll give you a chance to get on the road. He'll meet you there," Mulholland said.

Hays filled Lyons in on what Séan Mulholland had told her.

"Let's get out there sharpish. Those blaggards must still be in the area."

* * *

The Christmas frenzy of shopping for presents and cards was well underway in Galway. Even at that early hour of the morning, the streets were busy, and cars had been parked all over the place, ignoring the yellow lines and disabled space signs, so that navigating through the narrow streets was a chore. Several times Hays had to give a quick blast on his car's siren to get a vehicle to move out of the way, but at least the weather seemed to have taken pity on the shoppers. It was grey, overcast and breezy, but the rain was holding off, for now at least.

It took them a full hour to reach Roundstone, where commerce seemed to be moving at a more relaxed pace. They spotted Jim Dolan's squad car parked directly outside O'Dowds Pub, and Hays pulled his silver Mercedes in behind it.

"Good morning, Jim," Lyons said as she got out of the car.

"Morning, Inspector. You got here quickly," Dolan said.

"Yes, Mick doesn't hang about. And the car knows the way by now in any case," Lyons said.

The three Gardaí went inside O'Dowds, where the staff were cleaning the place and setting the bar up for the day ahead. Even in the depths of winter, O'Dowds enjoyed a reasonably brisk trade at lunch time, and again in the evening, although, of course, nothing like the number of customers that frequented the place in summer, when they often spilled out onto the street, and had to queue for their meal.

A bright young Polish girl came over when she saw the group entering the place.

"Good morning," she said with just a slight trace of an accent, "how may I help you this morning?"

Hays introduced the trio and asked if there was a manager around.

"Not yet, I'm afraid. He doesn't come on till half past twelve today. But I'm sure I can help you," she said confidently, "my name is Anika, and I'm in charge when the boss isn't here."

"OK, Anika, thank you. May I ask if you have any CCTV here?" Hays said.

Lyons was doing her usual trick. She had broken off from the little group and was having a good snoop around the public bar and lounge. Then she went out through the door at the back of the bar, where the premises opened up into a large kitchen and service area. She noticed that it appeared to be spotlessly clean. Two young men were working at the benches preparing salads and sauces for the lunchtime crowd.

"No, I'm sorry, Inspector, we just have a camera trained on the till for security reasons, but it doesn't pick up much – just the till itself. What is this about please?" Anika said.

"Sometime over the last couple of days, you took in some new €50 notes across the bar. They were in the lodgement that was made using the night safe in Clifden last night. I don't suppose you remember anything about that?" Hays asked.

"Well, yes, as a matter of fact I do. I was serving the night before last and these two guys came in and bought drinks. They weren't local. They paid for the first drinks with a new €50, and I gave them change, but when they got their next drinks, they paid again with another new €50 note. I remember it, because we were running low on twenties, and I couldn't understand why they didn't use the change I had given them," the girl said. "Did I do something wrong?"

"Oh no, not at all, Anika. But would you recognize these men again if you saw them?"

"Maybe. It was quite busy, and I wasn't really looking at their faces. I was concentrating on pulling their pints."

Hays took a sheet of paper with two photographs on it out of his inside pocket, and unfolded it on the counter in front of the girl.

"Could these be the men?" he said.

"Hmmm, yes, maybe. They look a little familiar, but I can't be sure. I'm sorry," Anika said.

Hays wasn't sure if the girl was just being careful not to identify the Geraghty brothers for fear of some unpleasantness down the line, or if she was being genuine.

"OK, Anika. Thanks for your help. Here's my card. If you see these two in here again, I want you to call me urgently. Don't let them see you making the call, just be sure to call immediately, won't you?"

"Yes, yes of course. Sorry I couldn't be more help," she said.

When Lyons re-appeared from her uninvited tour of the premises, the three sat into Dolan's squad car to compare notes.

"Anything Jim, Maureen?" Hays said.

"No, Mick. The place looks clean and well run, but I didn't spot anything unusual. The Geraghtys weren't hiding in the fridge anyway," she said.

"Jim?"

"I checked out the CCTV while you were talking to the girl. It's as she said. It's just a single camera focused on the till in the lounge. Not very high tech at all."

"Damn. Well at least we know that they are probably still in the area. That's something. Let's drop in on Pascal and see if he can at least give us a cup of tea," Hays said.

They drove out in the two cars to the little one-man Garda station near the church at the end of the village and parked.

"Morning Pascal," Lyons said as the three of them entered the station.

"Oh, good morning, Inspector. Morning Inspector Hays, Jim. To what do I owe the pleasure?" Brosnan said, looking just a little uncomfortable with the invasion by two senior officers and a colleague.

"Have you got the kettle on, Pascal? And I hope you have some biscuits," Lyons said.

"Oh, right. Just a pit-stop then. Any news on the Geraghtys?" Brosnan said as he refilled the kettle and rooted in the cupboard for some clean mugs and a packet of chocolate digestives.

"Well, we believe they were in O'Dowds the other night. They passed two more of Paddy McKeever's fifties across the bar. It might be a good idea if you were to

71

spend some time in O'Dowds yourself, Pascal. In plain clothes, of course," Hays said.

"Well that's no hardship, sir. I'll go down for my evening meal tonight and hang around for a while, see if anything turns up."

They were all seated at the small round table that occupied much of the floor space in the small kitchenette at the back of the station, when the sound of a tractor arriving in the car park got their attention.

Brosnan rose and looked out the window.

"That's old Cormac Fitzgerald. He's probably here about the tax on that tractor of his. It's ancient. I don't know how it keeps going at all," Brosnan said, moving back out to the public office at the front.

A few minutes later, Brosnan re-appeared and sat back down at the table.

"Now there's a funny one for ye," he said. "Old Fitzer came in to tell me that he was out late last night checking up on his sheep, and he swears he saw smoke coming from the chimney of the old cottage up the boreen behind the village; An Tigín it's called. And he was asking if that qualified him for the reward. Honest to God, I'm not joking!" Brosnan said.

"Is this old guy reliable?" Lyons asked.

"Oh, I'd say he is. He must be nearly eighty now, but he's as sharp as a needle," Brosnan said.

"And is his tractor taxed?" Dolan said.

"Ah well, he'll get that sorted out, don't worry. He was driving an old black Morris Minor up to a few weeks back, but it basically fell apart, so now he uses the tractor to get about, but it's not taxed for the road. So, I told him he needs to get that fixed up. It'll be fine, I'll make sure he does it," Brosnan said.

"And what about this Tigín place. Who owns it?" Lyons said.

"It used to belong to Festus O'Rourke. He died last year — remember? It was his grave where that bloke Weldon was found on the day of the funeral. Then some fancy fella from Galway bought the cottage. It's been empty ever since. He's looking to build a big extension onto it, and he has the planning permission lodged with the council. I doubt they'll go for it though, unless he can pull a few strings, the access is very poor," Brosnan said.

"Maybe we should wander up and have a look around. But not all of us, we don't want to be spotted. Why don't you go back into Clifden, Jim? Maureen and I will stroll up to the house and see if there's any sign of anything," Hays said.

"Do you think we should get backup out, Mick?" Lyons said.

"Not yet. Let's just have a look ourselves first. Plunkett would go completely crazy if we got the ARU out again for no reason," Hays said.

Chapter Twelve

Brosnan gave Hays and Lyons directions on how to get to An Tigín. They parked their car at the bottom of the narrow track, which had a healthy crop of grass and weeds growing up in the middle of it.

"We'd better put on our pistols, Maureen, just in case," Hays said.

The two detectives retrieved their Sig Sauer P220 handguns from the special cases in which they were stored in the boot of Mick Hays' car.

"I hope we don't need these things, I hate them," Lyons said, attaching the gun's holster to her belt, and pulling her jacket down over it, so as to keep it out of sight.

They sauntered up along the narrow, twisty track towards the cottage as if they were just having a look around, perhaps in the manner of some prospective buyers. They stopped to read the planning application nailed to the gate, and then moved on up the path towards the house itself. As they rounded the last bend, they spotted the dark green Pajero with the Galway registration plate parked outside the cottage.

Lyons went to the side of the vehicle, intending to see if the passenger's door was open, while Hays continued on up towards the front door of the house. It was in quite poor repair, with the dark green paint on the front door cracked and peeling, and the wooden window frames to the sides of the entrance rotting away slowly. He wasn't surprised. If it had been occupied by an old-timer who couldn't maintain the property in reasonable condition, and then been left idle for a year, it was hardly any wonder that the house needed some TLC.

Just as Hays got close to the front of the house, the door burst open. A man came running out, shotgun in hand, quickly followed by another man who was armed with a short iron crowbar. The man with the gun levelled it at Hays, and there was an almighty bang as the gun was discharged right at the inspector.

Hays keeled over where he stood, screaming and clutching at his thigh. The man ran on towards the vehicle, and seeing Maureen emerging from behind it, once again pointed his gun right at her. The second man shouted, "No! Leave her. We need to get outta here!"

Lyons fumbled with her jacket in an effort to release her side-arm from its holster, but by the time she had it in her hand, the old jeep had been started and was tearing off around the corner of the driveway, wheels spinning, throwing up gravel. Lyons aimed her pistol at the rear of the jeep, and just managed to get one shot away, smashing the back window, before the old Pajero, its engine roaring, disappeared around the corner.

Lyons ran to her partner.

"Mick, Mick, are you OK?"

Hays' trousers were shredded on his left leg above the knee, and blood was seeping out onto his hand where he was holding it. His eyes were squeezed tightly shut, and he was clearly in a great deal of pain, writhing on the ground in the dirt.

Lyons realised she needed to stem the blood flow, but how? She ran back into the house and grabbed a towel from the linen cupboard beside the old fireplace, and dashed back to his side. She folded the towel into a pad, and pressed it against his bleeding leg. Then she took off her belt and wrapped it around the leg, tightening it over the towel to exert pressure on the wound and hold it in place. The blood flow from his wound slowed.

"Christ, Mick. Stay with me. I'll get help."

Lyons took out her mobile phone and called Séan Mulholland.

"Séan, Séan, it's Maureen. Look, Mick has been shot. We're here at the old cottage up behind Roundstone, An Tigín it's called. I need an ambulance immediately. And get road blocks set up for the Pajero. The two Geraghtys are after getting clean away in it," Lyons barked down the phone.

"Jesus, Maureen. Is he OK? I'll get the ambulance out at once. But call Pascal. Get him to get the doctor from Roundstone. That'll be quicker."

Lyons then called Brosnan and told him what had happened, and asked him to get the doctor from the village up to the cottage as soon as possible.

Hays was still losing blood. After ten minutes, Lyons had to release the belt on his leg for a minute or two to minimize the damage to the blood vessels in his leg. When she did, blood started flowing from the wound again onto the ground, and Hays was going very cold and grey, and she felt he was slipping into unconsciousness.

"Mick. Mick! Stay with me. Talk to me!" she shouted, but all Hays could do was grunt and groan as the pain broke through following the original shock that he had suffered, which had initially suppressed the agony.

After what seemed an age, but was in fact only seven or eight minutes, a red Volvo estate car skidded to a halt on the loose gravel. Dr Brady, who had had the good sense to bring his nurse with him, climbed out and ran across to where the prone form of Senior Inspector Hays lay on the ground.

As he started to work on Hays, he introduced himself, and his nurse, Agnes.

Brady filled a syringe with a clear liquid and injected Hays in the good leg saying, "This will ease the pain. Agnes, get me a large dressing from my bag, and let's see if we can set up a drip here too. And get the rug from the back seat, he's very cold."

Brady removed the temporary arrangement that Lyons had fixed to Hays' leg with her belt. He then cut away Hays' trousers and peeled them back to reveal a number of pellet wounds in the man's leg. He applied a proper dressing to the wounds and strapped it on tightly to seal the wound. With the help of the nurse, he then set up a drip with a clear plastic bag full of fluid, asking Agnes to hold it two feet above Hays to allow gravity to feed the liquid into him.

"Maureen, can you go in the house and see if you can find a hot water bottle? He's very cold, and we don't want to add hypothermia to his troubles. Is the ambulance on its way?" the doctor said.

"Yes, I called it about fifteen minutes ago. I'll see to the hot water bottle."

Lyons was very reluctant to leave her partner again, but figured he was in good hands, and he needed to heat up. She went into the house and filled a kettle, putting it on the gas stove to warm while she searched for a hot water bottle.

As she moved around the dirty old kitchen, she noticed a half empty bottle of vodka on the table, and several empty beer bottles.

"They'll be great for fingerprints," she thought to herself, unable, despite the emergency, to get police procedure out of her head.

She found an old stone hot water bottle at the bottom of the hotpress beside the open hearth, and filled it with the water from the kettle which by now was singing nicely. She wrapped the stone jar in another old towel before bringing it back outside to where Hays was still lying on the ground.

Back outside the doctor was still kneeling on the rough ground attending to his patient. Lyons gave him the hot water jar, which he placed against Hays' side – the side away from the injury.

A few minutes later they heard the wailing of the ambulance's siren approaching. The ambulance driver squeezed his bright yellow vehicle past Dr Brady's Volvo and pulled up. The two paramedics got out of the ambulance and came trotting over, their kit bags in their hands.

"He's been shot," Dr Brady said to the ambulance crew, "he's lost a good bit of blood, but I've given him some morphine for the pain, and as you can see we have a saline drip up."

"Thanks, Doc," the senior paramedic said, "we'll take it from here. Deirdre, get his B.P. and SATS for me. Who put the towel on his leg?"

"That was me," Lyons said.

"Good work. You may just have saved his life," the man said.

Lyons turned away, tears welling in her eyes. She didn't realise how badly Mick had been injured by the shotgun blast.

Pascal Brosnan had arrived on foot, having parked his car further down the track to avoid blocking everyone in.

"How's Inspector Hays?" he asked Lyons when he saw the medics working on Hays on the ground.

"He's in good hands, but the bastards just shot him in cold blood. We have to find these two before they can cause any more damage. Can you get onto Séan and see what he can organise by way of a search party? And make sure all the local stations are well briefed. I'm going to get the forensics out to the house. The Geraghtys left in a hurry, so there's probably some good evidence in there. They may even have gone without the stolen cash. Are you firearms trained, Pascal?" Lyons said.

"I am, Inspector, but I don't have a weapon, and I don't want one either. I hate the damn things," the Garda replied.

Lyons walked off to a quiet spot at the side of the house and called Sinéad Loughran.

"Hi Sinéad. Look, I'm out here at Roundstone. Mick has been shot by the Geraghty brothers. He's OK, well sort of, there's a doctor and an ambulance here now. Can you get a team out here asap? The Geraghtys left in a hurry, and there'll be lots of forensic evidence in the house."

"God, Maureen, that's awful. Are you OK?" Loughran said.

"Bearing up, Sinéad. I have to go now, I'll text you the GPS co-ordinates of this place. Oh, and can you contact Eamon and Sally and put them in the picture. When I know where they are taking Mick, I'll call them."

"Yes, sure. What about the superintendent?" Loughran asked.

"He can wait till things have calmed down a bit. I'll call him in a while."

"OK. I'll see you soon, and Maureen, I'm really sorry," Loughran said and hung up.

Lyons walked back over to where the paramedics were attending to her partner. They now had Mick wrapped in a thermal blanket, and he had been placed on a stretcher.

"We're ready to put him in the ambulance now, Inspector. Are you coming with us?" the senior paramedic asked.

"Where are you taking him?"

"Well, he's stable now. His blood pressure is just about OK and we have managed to stop the bleeding, so I think we'll head straight into the Regional Hospital in Galway. We'll be there in forty minutes or so."

"OK. Thanks. I'll follow in Mick's car when I have seen to a few things here. Before you load him up, can I get his gun out of its holster? It needs to go back into the secure compartment in the boot of his car," Lyons said.

"Oh, yes, sure. But can you leave his belt on — just take the gun out, I don't want the bleeding to start again from disturbing him?"

"Yes, OK."

Lyons gently removed Hays' handgun from its holster, turned away, and emptied the chamber, removed the magazine of bullets, and made sure the safety catch was on, before placing it inside her jacket. She gave Mick's hand a squeeze, and then the paramedics lifted him into the back of the ambulance, closed it up, and departed with sirens blaring and blue lights flashing.

Lyons then thanked the doctor and his nurse for coming out so quickly.

"You must have just dropped everything, thank you so much. Were you in the middle of surgery?"

"Oh, don't worry, they'll keep. And they'll enjoy the drama. Not in any malicious way, you understand, but we haven't had anything like this happen out here before," Dr Brady said.

"Yes, well thanks anyway. Send your bill to me," Lyons said, handing him a business card.

"Oh, that won't be necessary, Inspector, there'll be no charge on this occasion."

The doctor and his assistant duly departed, and left Lyons there standing close to Mick Hays' spilt blood on the ground.

"Right, Pascal. I'm going to follow the ambulance back into town now. I need you to stay here on point until the forensic team and some more backup get here. But listen, I want you to take my gun. If this lot come back —

and they could easily if they have left the money in the house – you can't afford to be vulnerable," Lyons said.

"God, they hardly will, Inspector. I'll be fine."

"But take the gun anyway, Pascal. I couldn't bear it if another cop got shot on my watch. And if you get the chance, put one right between the eyes of that bastard – for me!"

She handed over her pistol along with the spare magazine that she had taken from Hays' weapon, giving Brosnan twenty rounds in all. If they did come back, even if he wasn't a great shot, that should give him enough ammunition to do some damage.

Chapter Thirteen

As Lyons drove back towards Galway, she telephoned Sally Fahy.

"Hi Sally, it's Maureen here. How are things?"

"Oh, hi Inspector. How are you, and how's Inspector Hays?"

Lyons filled the girl in on the latest developments, and asked Fahy to meet her with Eamon Flynn out at the Regional Hospital in about an hour. They needed to plan their next moves.

"And Inspector, the Super is going nuts. He's been down three times already. Maybe you should give him a call," Fahy said.

"OK. Will do. See you soon."

Lyons spent a few minutes getting the story clear in her head before calling Superintendent Finbarr Plunkett. He would probably not be best pleased that herself and Hays had gone to the house on their own, without backup, but she didn't think he would be too aggressive about it. In situations where the chips were down, as it were, he tended to be fairly supportive.

"Superintendent, it's Maureen Lyons," she said when he answered his phone on the first ring.

"Ah, Maureen. How are you, and how is Mick?"

"Well, he's on his way to the Regional Hospital in an ambulance. But he's stable according to the doctor who attended him at the house, and they reckon he'll be OK — eventually," she said.

"God, Maureen, that's awful. I'm sure he'll be fine. I haven't lost an officer in thirty-five years on the force you know," he said, as if that was a guarantee of some sort that he never would lose one.

He went on, "Any sign of the scoundrels that did this?"

"None, sir. I have all the available personnel out looking for them, and all the stations in the area have been alerted. Sinéad Loughran and her team are on the way out to the house where it happened, and Pascal Brosnan is on point. I gave him my gun in case they returned before back up arrives."

"Right, that's fine. We don't want any more shenanigans with those two. Were you hurt at all, Maureen?"

"No, sir. I was concealed behind a vehicle when they came roaring out of the house and just … sorry, sir," she said, unable to keep the emotion out of her voice.

"It's all right, Maureen, you've had a terrible shock," Plunkett said, not knowing quite how to deal with the woman.

"Oh, and there's one more thing, sir. I discharged my firearm. As they were escaping, I fired into the vehicle through the back window, but I don't think I hit anyone."

"Hmmm. Well don't write that up just yet, Maureen, we might put a bit of a different perspective on that in case it ever ends up with GSOC. Let me think about it."

"Right, sir. Thanks."

* * *

Galway Regional Hospital is located just at the end of the N59, the road that comes from Clifden and Roundstone into the city. When Lyons arrived, she asked at reception for the ward where Hays had been taken, and was informed that he had been taken directly to the operating theatre where Mr Michael O'Flaherty, a surgeon, was looking after him.

Lyons was directed to a family room on the second floor where she could wait, and get a much needed cup of coffee. The room was functional, yet cosy for a hospital. There was a sofa, two easy chairs, a small table with three kitchen style chairs tucked in around it, and in one corner there was a kettle, a microwave oven, and a tiny bright metal sink. A jar of instant coffee, a box of teabags and a carton of fresh milk sat beside the kettle, and an array of brightly coloured mugs were stacked there too. A large window looked out onto the university campus nearby, with its peculiar mixture of old and new buildings and extensive grass areas and playing fields.

Lyons brewed a cup of strong coffee, and then called Sally Fahy giving her directions to the room in which she was waiting.

"Do you want me to bring a sandwich for you, or something, Inspector?" Fahy asked before hanging up.

"No, it's OK thanks, I've no appetite at all, and if I do get hungry, I can get something here, thanks."

Ten minutes later, the three detectives were seated around the little table in the family room.

"OK folks. Let's look at what we know so far. These thugs rob the postman, killing him in the process, and get away with sixty thousand euro and change. They then swap their old Mondeo for a jeep at Deasy's, but why do they not get out of the area? It doesn't make sense to me. In their new vehicle, they could easily have got through, or they could have split up and we'd never have caught them," Lyons said.

"You think there's a reason why they have hung around?" Flynn said.

"I don't know Eamon, it just seems odd. Anyway, what else have we got? Anything on the car?" Lyons asked.

"Sinéad gave it a good going over. Lots of prints, and you know about the wrapper from the money. There was an empty vodka bottle on the floor in the back, and apart from that, not much else. A few receipts for fuel from various petrol stations in the area, that's about it," Sally said.

"Who was the vehicle registered to?" Lyons asked.

Fahy and Flynn exchanged a nervous glance.

"An Garda Síochána," Flynn said, trying to keep a straight face.

"For God's sake! How the hell did that happen?" Lyons said.

"It seems when it was sold off, we didn't do the paperwork, or at least not properly. They must have assumed it was going for scrap. It was never transferred to the new owner," Flynn said.

"Sloppy – very sloppy. Which means it won't have any parking tickets or speeding offences registered against it. I wonder if they knew?" Lyons said.

"I doubt it. I'd say they just bought it from some dodgy dealer, cash in hand somewhere. It wasn't up to much anyway," Flynn said.

There was a knock at the door, and a nurse came in.

"Ms Lyons?" the nurse said.

"Yes, that's me."

"Mr Hays is out of surgery now. You can see him for a few minutes if you like. He's a bit woozy after the anaesthetic, but he's awake – kind of."

Lyons walked down what seemed like an endless set of corridors till she reached room 212A, a private room close to the lifts.

"Well, look at you," she said as she entered and went to his bedside.

"Hi Maureen," he mumbled, and she bent over the bed and hugged him as tightly as she could. Her tears flowed freely as she clung to him, and he held her closely for several minutes.

"Bloody hell, Hays, you sure know how to scare a girl. And what made you think you were Mr Invincible anyway?" she said, sitting down in the chair beside the bed and gripping his hand tightly.

"That's more like it! Nothing about how are you, or does it hurt?" he said.

"I bet it does," she said.

"And did we get the little buggers?" he said.

"'Fraid not. I did manage to shoot out the back window of their jeep mind you. I don't think Plunkett is too pleased about that. But they got away. We have a big man hunt going on, so we may get them soon enough. How long will you be in here?" she said.

"Just a day or two. They boot out as many as they can this week with Christmas coming. I'll probably be on crutches for a week or two. But they say it will heal up pretty well. They took thirty-two lead pellets out of my leg, and apparently they missed an artery by a whisker. Thanks, by the way."

"What for?"

"For saving my life with your belt. I heard the doctor say it as I was lying on the ground out there." He squeezed her hand.

"Ah, go on will ye. When I took it off, I was going to whip your backside for being such an idiot, but then I decided I'd better try and stop the bleeding instead," she said, smiling.

"Did they get my gun?"

"No, not at all. I removed it when you were being put in the ambulance. It's in the safe in your car boot. I had to give mine to Pascal Brosnan in the hope that the Geraghtys would come back to the house and he could shoot them both."

The nurse came back in to the room.

"That's enough for now, Ms Lyons. He needs to rest. You can come back later if you like. Visiting is from six to eight thirty."

As Lyons was getting up, she said, "OK. I'll see you later. Is there anything you need brought in?"

"A pair of pyjamas wouldn't go amiss, and maybe a toothbrush and shaving kit."

"Right, will your pink ones with the sequins be OK? I think the others are in the wash."

"Perfect!"

The nurse gave them both a strange look.

Lyons found her way back to the family room and asked the two detectives to go back to the station and follow things up from there.

Chapter Fourteen

When she got to the house Hays and herself shared in Salthill, Lyons called the station and spoke to Sally Fahy.

"Any news on the two louts?" Lyons said.

"Not a whisper I'm afraid, they've gone to ground again."

"So, what are we doing about it?"

"Well, Sinéad and her guys have spent most of the afternoon out at the house. She's just been on the phone, and she's coming back in now. They found quite a bit of forensic evidence it seems, but no money. But they found a half empty box of cartridges. She says she may be able to trace where they were bought from the batch number on the box. And she got loads of fingerprints and DNA, so when we find them they'll be for the high jump," Fahy said.

"I'm glad you said 'when', Sally, not 'if'. But what I can't understand is why they haven't scarpered away out of there. Why are they hanging around?" Lyons said.

"God knows. I have no idea how their nasty little minds work. Are you coming back in?" Fahy said.

"No. I'm at home getting Mick some stuff, and then I'll be going back to the hospital. I'll be in first thing tomorrow though. Can you arrange a meeting for nine?" Lyons said.

"Yes, sure. Oh, and by the way, Superintendent Plunkett was looking for you."

"Oh, right, I'll give him a call later. Thanks. See you tomorrow."

* * *

Lyons gathered up a bag of toiletries, a pair of plain navy pyjamas, socks, underpants and a clean pair of trousers, and put them all in a small green holdall. She managed to squeeze in Hays' dressing gown too, and then she tidied up the house and put things away neatly before leaving again for the hospital.

They were just serving tea when she arrived back in, and the nurse looking after Hays went and got a spare cup for Lyons.

"You're looking a bit better, Mick. You've got some colour back in your cheeks. How are you feeling?" Lyons said.

"A bit easier. They've got me on some pretty strong pain killers, so I feel a bit out of it, but at least there's no real discomfort. Those shotgun pellets hurt like hell."

Lyons then outlined what they were doing to try and find the Geraghtys, and asked Hays if he had any ideas, as they seemed to be getting nowhere in their search.

"Tell you what. Why don't I see if Rollo will meet you? He seems to have some connection to this lot's information, and he may know something," Hays said.

"Bit of a long shot, don't you think? And his last tip off was a good bit wide of the mark."

"I know, but still, he might have heard something. And he'll be keen to help after his last bit of information was so wrong. I'll leave a message in that terrible dump of a pub he drinks in, if you're up for it?" Hays said.

"OK, if you think it might help. I don't mind meeting him," Lyons said.

Lyons stayed with Hays for another hour, chatting about nothing of any great importance. She could see by then that he was getting very tired. The medication was clearly making him drowsy, and the nurse had said that sleep was the best cure at this stage, so Lyons kissed him goodnight and left the room.

Outside the room, Sinéad Loughran was seated on a chair in the corridor.

"Hi, Sinéad, what's up?" Lyons said, quite surprised to see the woman there.

"I just dropped in to see how he is, but when I saw you were in there, I waited here," Loughran said.

"Ah, that was kind of you. He's doing OK, but he's just going off to sleep right now," Lyons said, feeling awkward that she was putting Sinéad off going into Hays' room when she had been kind enough to come all the way out to the hospital to see him.

"That's OK. I can see him tomorrow. There's a lot of people at the station feeling very concerned about him, you know. Anyway, what about you? When did you last eat?" Loughran said.

"God, I can't remember. Now that you mention it, I am a bit peckish."

"Right. Well let's go and get something to eat then. Where do you fancy?" Loughran said.

"To be honest, I just want to get home. It's been a hell of a day, and I'm all in," Lyons said.

"OK. Well then this is what we'll do. I'll drive you home and I'll rustle up something for us to eat. You can have a soak in the tub while I'm cooking, and then I'll leave you to it."

"It's OK, Sinéad, I'll be fine," Lyons said.

"Nonsense, I insist. And we can stop on the way and pick up a bottle of wine. Let's go!"

* * *

When they got back to Lyons' house, she went straight away to run the bath as Sinéad Loughran had instructed, while Sinéad herself started on the cooking.

Lying in the warm bubbly water, Lyons replayed the events of the day over in her head.

Obviously, they had been foolish to approach the two brothers in the house without any backup, but if they had called out armed response again, and the cottage had turned out to be empty, then they would have been given a terrible time for wasting money by the superintendent. But maybe they should have been a bit more subtle in their approach to the house.

Anyway, she couldn't change the past. What she needed to do now was to show some leadership. Organise the team and the other resources at her disposal, and flush out the two thugs before anyone else got hurt. But how? They could be absolutely anywhere, and Christmas week wasn't exactly the best time to ensure maximum focus on things. Damn! She could do with Mick operating at full strength to get them out of this mess – but that wasn't going to happen either – not for a while at least. "Damn, damn, damn," she said to herself, topping up the bath with some more hot water.

* * *

Downstairs, Sinéad had prepared a nice meal of pasta carbonara with a fresh green salad, and had opened the bottle of Campo Viejo they had bought in the local convenience store on the way home.

"Wow. Thanks, Sinéad, that looks gorgeous. And you're right, I'm starving!" Lyons said when she saw the spread laid out on the kitchen table.

The two women tucked into the meal in silence, topping up their wine glasses until the bottle was empty. Lyons was feeling better already.

"So, what are your plans for Christmas?" Sinéad said.

"We were going to go to my sister's up in Athenry like we did last year, but to be honest, I doubt if we will now with Mick injured. We'll probably just have a quiet time at home here. The sister's place is a bit mad anyway. She has four young kids, and her husband will probably have to work. They have what used to be the family farm, and there always seems to be loads to do. Animals don't stop just 'cos it's Christmas. And they usually have Aunt Maude there too. She's as nutty as a fruit cake, and a bit gaga, so maybe it's just as well we're giving it a miss. What about you?" Lyons said.

"I'll go home to my folks' place in Loughrea. It will just be my brother and me and the parents. Very boring, but Mam puts on a good spread, and the whole thing is very understated," Sinéad said.

"What does your brother do?" Lyons said.

"He works for the local council at something or other. I know – I should take more interest, but whatever he does it's monumentally boring, that much I do know."

"Will you get any nice presents?" Lyons said.

"I suppose I'll get some crappy scarf from Aidan – I have about ten of them already, and I never wear any of them. Why do people buy such shite at Christmas?" They both laughed.

"What will you get for Mick?" Sinéad asked.

"Oh, he's been angling for a new, and quite expensive sailing jacket. A Musto or something. Bloody thing costs about €150, but I can't think of anything else."

"And what will you get from him?" Sinéad said.

"Probably nothing this year, at least until he's up and about again. But he's pretty good with presents. I think he fancies the young one in Hartman's jewellery shop in town. In fairness she is gorgeous – Monika – she's Polish. He's always in there buying me stuff, so I can't complain really," Lyons said.

Sinéad couldn't help but be a little envious of Maureen. Sinéad herself never seemed to want to settle with any of the men she had met so far, and at 34, her biological clock was definitely ticking. But Mr Right had eluded her, and she wasn't prepared to settle for just anyone. "Too fussy, maybe," she often thought to herself.

The two girls opened a second bottle of red wine and made good inroads into it chatting about all sorts of things. They got on well, and before they realised, it was eleven o'clock.

"You'd better stay over, Sinéad," Lyons said when they realised how late it was, "Besides, you've had too much drink to drive. There's fresh linen on the bed in the spare room, and it has an electric blanket. You'll be fine there," Lyons said.

"OK. Thanks a million, Maureen," Loughran said, finishing her glass of wine.

Sinéad went upstairs to have a wash and get ready for bed while Lyons tidied away their plates and cutlery and did a quick clean up around the kitchen, putting all the dirty stuff in the dishwasher.

A few minutes later, both women were tucked up for the night. Lyons lay awake for some time, going over the events that had led to her partner being nearly killed. A cold shiver went down her spine when she remembered him lying in the dirt, the lifeblood oozing out of his damaged leg. She wondered if there wasn't some easier career that they could both pursue, with less chance of getting killed at work, and as she drifted off to sleep, unpleasant images flitted across her mind.

Chapter Fifteen

The following morning, Sinéad drove Lyons back to the hospital where she had left her car overnight. Sinéad didn't go in, but Lyons did, just to see Hays for a minute to make sure that he was OK and had spent a comfortable night.

She looked in through the little window of room 212A. Mick was sitting up in the bed finishing his breakfast. Lyons went in.

"Hi, you're looking a bit perkier," she said to Hays as he smiled warmly at her.

"Hi you. Thanks for coming in. Are you on your way to work?"

"Yeah. Sinéad was here last night just as I was leaving, so she drove me home and we had some grub. She stayed over," Lyons said.

"Oh, I didn't see her. Tell her thanks for coming in."

"She said she might stop by later. So, what have they got lined up for you today?" Lyons said.

"Well, as soon as the physio gets here, they're going to get me up and see if I can walk around a bit."

"Nice. I hope it's not too sore," she said holding his hand.

"Nah, it'll be fine. Now why don't you get off to work and don't worry about me. See if you can nail those bastards before I get out of here."

"Yeah, OK, I'll stop by later. Do you need anything?" Lyons said.

"No, I'm fine thanks. See you later." They kissed briefly before she left.

* * *

Lyons got into the station just before nine. She got a cup of coffee from the kitchen, and took it into the open plan where the rest of the team were already assembled.

As she stood at the whiteboard that had pictures of Paddy McKeever and the Geraghty brothers pinned up, she was conscious that everyone was looking to her to provide some inspiration about the case. For the first time in a long time, she actually felt nervous.

"Right," Lyons said, clearing her throat, "what have we got? Eamon?"

Eamon Flynn shifted nervously in his seat.

"Nothing, boss. I thought you might have something," he said rather sheepishly.

"Sally, have you anything? Anything at all?" Lyons said.

"Sorry, Inspector. They've been searching all over the place out near the cottage, but there's no sign of them. Not a trace," she said.

Lyons swallowed hard before she spoke.

"Right. This is what we're going to do. I want the search team out there increased. I want every single house in the area checked, and then re-checked. Eamon, will you

98

get onto Séan Mulholland and get him to put every available man he can spare on it? Tell him overtime is no problem, and tell him leave is cancelled till we find these two – except for Christmas Day and St Stephen's Day that is."

Lyons judged the mood amongst her colleagues before pressing on.

"And I want all of you to give your snouts a good rattle. There will be some word on the grapevine as to what's going on, and a lot of the lowlife we deal with don't go along with shooting Gardaí, so it may be possible to get some information there. Use every contact you can find. Right – let's get to it. If nothing breaks, we'll meet back here at five," she said with as much authority as she could muster.

* * *

Hays had done better with the physio than he had hoped. He was able to get in and out of bed unaided, and he could even walk around without a stick, provided he could hold onto things. The physiotherapist was well pleased, and confirmed that he could go home that evening, as long as there was someone available to dress the wound every day for another four or five days till it healed up. Hays assured her that he had a partner who would be happy to oblige, hoping that Maureen would step up to the job.

He was tired after the exertions, and was just dozing off in the late morning before the lunch came around, when to his surprise, Superintendent Finbarr Plunkett arrived in to see him.

"God Mick, how the hell are ya?" he said, full of cheer.

99

"Hello Superintendent, it's good of you to come in to see me. How are you keeping yourself?"

"It's Finbarr now Mick, no need to stand on ceremony, or even lie down on ceremony," he said, chuckling at his own joke.

Plunkett sat down in the visitor's chair, and tenuously brought the conversation around to the events that had put Hays in hospital in the first place.

"You see, Mick, I've had a call from The Park. Internal Affairs don't you know. They're keen to understand how this all came about, and the fact that Inspector Lyons fired off a shot has complicated things a bit. Now I think we can handle it all right, don't worry, and it's important that we do in view of the plans we have for the unit. But there'll be some difficult questions to answer, that's for sure," the superintendent said.

"I see. Like what for instance, Finbarr?"

"Like what the bloody hell you two were doing confronting two armed suspects without any backup – that sort of thing. Do you see what I mean?"

"Ah, look, it wasn't like that. We only had the flimsiest of information that there was anyone up at the house. And I was damned if I was going to get the ARU out just on the off chance after the fiasco out at Clifden. We were just doing a recce on the place when it all went to shit," Hays said.

"And what about Ms Smarty Pants firing one off into the back of the jeep? How are we going to explain that?"

"She says she saw the shotgun being poked out through the passenger's window of the Pajero, and she feared for her own safety and for mine, so she got her retaliation in first, if you see what I mean. Anyway, it worked."

"Ah, right. Well that sounds kind of feasible, I suppose. It's a good job she's a lousy shot! It just depends on who they send down, and what sort of an agenda he has. I'll know later who's coming, and I'll do some checking around to see what way the land lies. You might polish up that version of events a bit with Lyons before they start asking awkward questions. It sounds fairly OK to me," Plunkett said.

"Do you think we'll be all right, boss?"

"Ah, we'll do our best anyway, Mick. I've survived worse, believe me. It just depends what yer man is like. Some of those fellas have to find a scapegoat to blame, and some of the rest of them are pretty relaxed. We'll see. You get some rest, and get yourself back in after Christmas. I'll leave you to it now," Plunkett said, getting up to leave.

* * *

Lyons was just sitting down at her desk when her phone rang.

"This is Rollo," said the husky voice at the other end of the phone. "I had a call from Mr Hays. Do you want to meet?"

"Oh yes, eh... Rollo. Where? When?"

"Half an hour. Usual place. And bring me a nice Christmas present."

Hays had briefed Lyons that she would need a bottle of Powers Whiskey and €50 in small notes when she met Rollo, so she had no time to waste. She dashed out of the warm Garda station into the cold and wet of the street to get her 'gifts' for Rollo before retrieving her car and heading out to Salthill.

Lyons didn't know what to expect when she met Mick's favourite snout. She had heard him talk about this Rollo, but she had no idea what he looked like, or how he would behave towards her. She parked up along the promenade in Salthill, and walked nervously towards the concrete shelter, her body bent over against the strong, moist wind.

* * *

Rollo was seated inside the shelter backed up against one side wall in an attempt to make himself invisible. He was more of a down and out than she had expected. His clothes were old, filthy and torn and threadbare in places, and the soles of his shoes were parting company with the uppers, revealing a very dirty pair of socks full of holes. Lyons hadn't expected sartorial elegance, but this man was more like a tramp than an informant.

Lyons sat down a good two feet away from him, but could still get the strong whiff of stale body odour and pee from the man. Her stomach turned over, but somehow she managed not to show it.

"How's himself?" Rollo said.

"He's in hospital, but he'll be OK," Lyons said rather glumly.

"Sorry to hear that. Did you bring me my pressie?"

Lyons slipped the bottle of whiskey out from under her coat, and Rollo's scrawny, filthy hand reached out and took it, opening the screw cap and taking a good swig of the amber liquid.

"Ah, that's good. So, what do you want?" he said.

"Information. You know what happened. We're looking for the two clients. Have you heard anything about where they might be hiding out?" Lyons asked.

"Well, I don't think they're back in the town yet anyways. They must be still out there somewhere," the man said, and took another good measure of the whiskey.

"Is that it?" Lyons said. She wasn't warming to this man at all. She felt very uncomfortable, and the smell was overpowering. She wanted to go.

"Maybe I heard a bit more," he said.

Lyons looked at him, and then the penny dropped. She slipped the five used ten euro notes across. Rollo snatched the money quickly, and it disappeared from sight immediately.

"Glen. Glen something, or something Glen. I just heard a couple of blokes talking. I think they know them boys. But I couldn't get no more. I'm risking my life telling you this, you know," Rollo said.

"Damn it, Rollo, that's not much to go on, is it?" Lyons said.

"It's all I got. Take it or leave it."

Lyons got up to leave, giving the snout a long look.

"Tell Mr Hays I was asking after him now, won't ye?" Rollo said.

"Hmph," Lyons said and walked back to her car.

Chapter Sixteen

Inspector Frank Nicholson sat down opposite Superintendent Finbarr Plunkett in the superintendent's office.

"Sit down, Inspector, can I get you some coffee or tea?" the superintendent said.

"No, thanks, I'm fine."

"Good drive down?" the superintendent went on, trying hard to break the ice.

Frank Nicholson looked more like an expensive solicitor than a Garda from Internal Affairs. He had neatly trimmed salt and pepper hair, a lean, angular face, with narrow eyes and almost no lips at all. He was dressed in a very sharp grey suit, with an impeccably ironed pale-yellow shirt and navy tie. Despite the inclement weather, his black leather lace up shoes shone like beacons in the dull late afternoon light, and his hands were beautifully manicured. Before he replied, he took out a brown leather-bound notebook and gold Mont Blanc pen, and placed them carefully on the desk in front of him.

"Well, the weather deteriorated the further west I got," he said in a manner that made Finbarr Plunkett think it had to be his fault, "but I made good time all the same."

"And where are you staying tonight?" the superintendent said.

"They booked me into the Imperial, but I changed to the G," Nicholson said.

The superintendent said nothing, but raised his eyebrows in response. The Imperial was a good, modestly priced commercial hotel right in the city centre, whereas the G was a very upmarket boutique style place, festooned with expensive artworks. For some, it was considered *the* place to stay when in Galway.

"So, what have you been told about this incident then, Inspector?" Plunkett said.

"Just an outline of events. I'll need to speak to the officers involved as soon as possible, but I understand one of your men was hit with a shotgun blast while pursuing two potential killers more or less on his own. Is that right?" Nicholson said.

"No, not really. I'll let you get the real story directly from the officers involved, but you should know that they were not in pursuit at all, they were simply following up a very tenuous lead about some unusual activity at what should have been a deserted property," Plunkett said.

"I see. And are you saying that they were completely unaware that two armed and dangerous suspects were hiding out at the property?" said Nicholson, writing notes in his notebook.

"I believe that is the case. But, as I said, I'd rather you spoke to them yourself. What I'm telling you is only hearsay, and therefore not relevant," Plunkett said, keen not to implicate himself in any way, given the attitude of the man from Internal Affairs.

"I understand Senior Inspector Hays is still in hospital. When is he getting out, do you know?"

"He may already be home by now. They were releasing him today. And his partner, Inspector Lyons, is probably downstairs as we speak."

"Right, could you give him a call and see if he would be available for an interview tomorrow morning? I can call out to his house if that makes it a bit easier," Nicholson said, showing an unusual degree of empathy for the wounded officer – or did he just want to snoop around Hays' house?

The superintendent said nothing, but picked up the phone and called Mick Hays' mobile.

"Hello Mick. How are you feeling?" Plunkett said when Hays answered.

"And are you home now?"

Hays confirmed that he was at home.

"Well that's good anyway. Listen, I have Inspector Nicholson from I.A. here with me. He was wondering if you could be available for an interview tomorrow morning? He can come out to your house if you like."

"Oh, right. Yes, I understand, of course. Ten o'clock you say. Hold on a second," Plunkett said.

Nicholson nodded.

"Ten it is then, here in Mill Street. You can use my office. What? Oh, right, the ground floor, yes of course. I'll reserve a room for you both down below so. Thanks Mick. All the best," Plunkett said.

Nicholson stood up.

"Well, if that's all, Superintendent, I'll get out to my hotel and check in. I'll see you in the morning, perhaps."

"Fair enough, Inspector. Would you like me to stop by the G and we could have a drink later?" Plunkett said.

"No, you're fine, Superintendent. I have a good bit of paperwork to get done tonight. I'll see you tomorrow."

The two men shook hands, and Nicholson departed.

As soon as Nicholson had left and was out of earshot, Plunkett called Lyons at her desk.

"Maureen. If you have a minute, we need to talk," he said.

* * *

When Lyons got back to her desk having spoken to Superintendent Plunkett, she was very unsettled. From what Plunkett had told her, it looked as if this Inspector Nicholson was out for blood. Maybe that's what got you promoted in Internal Affairs, or maybe the man was just vindictive – it didn't matter, the result would be the same.

"Damn it," she said to herself, "if only I hadn't fired off my gun at the departing jeep, they would probably never have got involved."

She was pondering all sorts of dire scenarios in her head, when her phone rang.

"Lyons."

"Maureen, its Seán here out in Clifden."

"Hi, Seán. What's up?"

"We found the old green Pajero, Maureen. It's been burned out, but there's a good lot of it still intact. It's out near Murvey stuck in the old ruined barn beside where that fella Maguire used to live. Remember, the man we got for the murder of the Polish girl?" Mulholland said.

"Nice one, Séan. Yes, I remember the place well. How the hell did you find it?"

"Well, at this time of year we do the rounds of the places where the local men distil their poitín. They're often active coming up to Christmas, there's a good market for the stuff at this time of year. Peadar was out there hoping to catch them. He overheard an old fella in the pub saying he had seen smoke which he assumed was from a still, but when he went out to investigate, he found the jeep."

"OK, well I'll get Sinéad out to see what she can get off it. I don't suppose there was any cash in it?" Lyons said.

"Ah now, away with ye, Maureen. Fat chance."

Lyons called Sinéad Loughran and told her of Mulholland's find, asking her to get out there to see what they could get off the old jeep, and to confirm that it was definitely the one used by the two Geraghty brothers.

"Are you coming out too, Maureen?" Sinéad asked.

"No, no I'm not. Get Eamon to go with you. I need to be here. Mick is out of hospital and needs minding at home."

* * *

When Lyons got home she found Hays in good form. He seemed to be largely mobile, albeit with a pronounced limp, and he had prepared a meal for them both, complete with Maureen's favourite red wine – Valpolicella - which was served at just the right temperature.

"God, this is great, Mick. We must try and get you shot a bit more often if this is the result!"

As they ate their meal, Hays asked if Lyons had made contact with Rollo.

"Oh, yes I did. Crikey, Mick, you sure know how to pick them! He stank!" Lyons said between mouthfuls.

"I know he's no oil painting. But we have talked about that before. He says old fellas like him are completely invisible to most people. They just never see him, and that gives him the chance to eavesdrop on all sorts. Did he tell you anything that could help us with the Geraghtys?"

"He said he heard some blokes talking about them, and that the word 'Glen' came up in the conversation. That's all he knew," Lyons said.

"Is that all? And that cost you fifty euro!"

"No, Mick, it cost you fifty euro – and a bottle of whiskey. You can pay me later," she said smiling.

After they had finished eating, and polished off the bottle of wine, they sat over on the sofa in front of the fire.

"Glen, Glen," mused Hays. "Have you a map of Clifden and the nearby surroundings?"

"I think so. It's upstairs, hang on I'll go and get it," Lyons said.

Lyons came back a few minutes later with Ordnance Survey sheet number 37 covering Clifden and its environs to the north, and spread it out on the coffee table.

Hays leaned forward, wincing slightly as the muscles in his thigh were stretched.

They studied the map for a few minutes.

"The only thing I can see with 'Glen' associated with it in that area is the Abbey Glen Hotel," Hays said.

"That's funny. I was just looking at the Tribune earlier, and I saw an ad for a Stephen's Day party that they're holding out there. Apparently, it's an annual event.

Tickets are €20, and I was actually wondering if you might like to go. My treat," Lyons said.

"Well, maybe. But more importantly, if they have a big bash on Stephen's night, that means they'll have a right lot of cash to lodge the day after. And what's more, with the banks closed from Christmas Eve, they'll have all the takings from Christmas Eve night and Christmas Day as well," Hays said.

"Are you thinking what I'm thinking?" Lyons said.

"I sure am. Tell you what. After we have both had a nice chat with Inspector Nicholson tomorrow, why don't we head out there and have a talk to the manager. You can find out who he is in the morning and give him a call. Say we're coming out to see him," Hays said.

Chapter Seventeen

When Lyons arrived at Mills Street the following morning, Frank Nicholson was already there. He was looking even more dapper than he had the previous day, in a different navy pinstripe suit, the creases in the trousers of which were like blades.

"Come in, Inspector Lyons, this shouldn't take too long," Nicholson said with no hint of a smile.

They sat opposite each other in the small interview room. Lyons was glad that she had collected a cup of coffee from the Costa Coffee outlet across from the police station on her way in. Nicholson had none.

The man took out his leather-bound notebook and gold Mont Blanc pen, and prepared to take notes.

"I'd like you to outline the series of events that led up to the moment when you found it necessary to discharge your firearm out near Roundstone, Inspector," he said.

Lyons began, picking up the story from when Hays and herself had approached the house on foot.

"No, Inspector. I'd like you to start from the point where you were in the Roundstone Garda Station when the civilian came in and told you that there was someone occupying Tigín."

"Well, Inspector, firstly he said no such thing. He simply said that he thought that he had observed smoke coming from that direction, and he had surmised that it was from someone lighting a fire in the house," Lyons said.

"And did it not occur to Senior Inspector Hays or yourself that this might be where the Geraghtys were hiding out?" Nicholson asked.

"You'll have to ask Senior Inspector Hays what he thought when he was told of the smoke. I simply felt that it might be worth going up there to see if there was any actual evidence that someone was using the house."

"Was that not a bit naive of you?"

"If that is your judgement, then so be it," Lyons replied.

"Go on. What happened when you got to the cottage?"

Lyons went on to describe how both of them had approached the house, and as they did so, two men burst out the front door, the one in front brandishing a sawn-off shotgun which he fired at Hays, hitting him in the leg.

"And what did you do, Inspector?"

"I took cover to the side of the vehicle, and started removing my sidearm from its holster on my belt."

"Did you intend to shoot the fleeing gunman?"

"No, I did not. I intended to defend myself and protect Senior Inspector Hays as best I could in the event that there were any further attempts by the gunmen to do us harm."

"And were there?"

"Yes. As the jeep sped off, I saw the barrel of the shotgun appear out of the passenger's side window of the vehicle, pointed in our direction. So, in order to deter the gunman from firing again, I put a single round from my pistol into the rear of the jeep. It appears that it had the desired effect, as the gunman didn't shoot again," Lyons said.

"When you fired your gun, did you intend to kill or wound either of the occupants of the fleeing vehicle?"

"No. That was not my intention. As I have said, I fired into the vehicle as a deterrent, and it seems to have been a successful one."

"I presume you have returned the gun to the armoury here, and that the bullets have been counted back?" Nicholson said.

"No, Inspector, I haven't returned it yet. In fact, I lent it to Garda Pascal Brosnan as he was left on point at the property. I gave it to him to defend himself in case the gunmen returned. As they left in a hurry, I thought they might come back looking for something that they had left at the house, and without a gun, Brosnan would have been a sitting duck."

"And tell me, Inspector, do you normally just give away your firearm to anyone you casually meet whom you think might find it useful?"

"I was hoping to find another criminal to give it to, Inspector, but as they had all disappeared, I gave it to a firearm trained member of the force instead," Lyons said, beginning to get very fed up with the way the interview was going.

"Now, if there's nothing else, Inspector Nicholson, I have two potential cop killers to run to earth," Lyons said.

"Very well, Inspector. We'll leave it at that – for now," Nicholson said.

Lyons got up, turned and left the room without another word.

When she got back to her desk, she called Hays on his mobile. He was on the way to the station in his car. Lyons relayed the details of the discussion she had had with Inspector Frank Nicholson, and they agreed that he would tell exactly the same story, which was, in any case, for the most part perfectly accurate.

When Hays went into the interview room to have his discussion with Nicholson, he exaggerated the extent of his wound somewhat. The interview went much the same as Lyons', with Hays just adding that at the time he feared for his life, and had it not been for Inspector Lyons, he might well have been shot again by the fleeing gunmen, with fatal consequences.

Nicholson finished the interview by ten thirty, and was slipping out of the station when the desk sergeant, Sergeant Flannery, caught his attention.

"Eh, I think the superintendent would like a word before you go, sir," Flannery said.

Nicholson pretended not to hear, but to his surprise, found that he couldn't open the outer door of the Garda station. Flannery had popped the electronic lock from behind his desk, so that Nicholson had to come back in.

"The outer door seems to be locked, Sergeant. I need to leave," he said.

"Ah, yes, right. It gets stuck a bit from time to time, but as I was saying, Superintendent Plunkett would like a word before you go. You can go right on up — you know where his office is."

Nicholson made his way up to Superintendent Plunkett's office, and knocked on the door.

"Come in, Inspector, come in. Would you like a cup of coffee, I'm just about to have one myself?"

"No thanks. I need to be getting back. This is the last working day before the holidays, and I need to get my report written up," Nicholson said.

"Oh, right. And how did that all go? Anything interesting come up?"

"I'm afraid I can't discuss it, Superintendent. I'll be writing it up, and sending it on to the chief superintendent. You'll hear all about it in due course."

"Well, it's usual in these cases, Inspector, to give a senior officer a 'heads-up' you know. It's important for me to know how to deal with my own officers. It's a sensitive situation."

"I'm sorry, Superintendent, I have my procedures to follow. I'll see that you are informed without delay," Nicholson said.

"Very well. You had better be on your way then. But Inspector Nicholson…"

"Yes?"

"Make sure you stay within the speed limit on the way back. My lads are very sharp with the speed traps on that road."

With that, the superintendent put his head down and went back to shuffling papers on his desk, leaving Nicholson to exit his office without further ceremony.

Hays and Lyons were back in Hays' office comparing notes.

"How do you think that went?" Lyons asked.

"I'm not sure. I'm sure we said more or less the same things, but I got no feedback at all from him. Seemed like a cold fish to me. What did you think?" Hays said.

"Same. He did make some smart-arsed remark about me lending my gun to Pascal, so I went back at him on that. Apart from that it was pretty straightforward. It just depends on his own agenda, I guess. We'll just have to wait and see. Now, are you up for a trip to the Abbey Glen?"

"Yeah, sure. Just let me check in with Plunkett first. Then we'll head off," Hays said.

Hays called the superintendent and they exchanged a few choice words about the man from Internal Affairs.

"I'd say we'll be all right, Mick. He can't make too much of it, to be honest, and with a bit of luck, the chief super will give me a heads-up before anything is cast in stone. Don't you worry about it in any case. Have a good Christmas, and let's hope we sort out the Geraghtys as soon as we're back," Plunkett said.

"Same to you, sir. And we have a bit more on that front. We may get it sorted sooner than we think," Hays said.

"Good man, Mick. That's the spirit. And give Maureen my best," Plunkett said finishing the conversation.

* * *

The two detectives set off for the Abbey Glen Hotel in Clifden. The traffic in town was manic, but once they

116

got past the university, things thinned out remarkably, and they encountered very few hold-ups as they drove out along the N59.

The weather was grey and overcast – the kind of atmosphere that renders the landscape flat and uninteresting, though the rain was holding off well. They passed Moycullen where the shopkeepers were busy raking in the very last of the Christmas trade, and then on out to Oughterard which seemed eerily quiet given the day that was in it.

"This place is like a ghost town," Lyons remarked as they drove along the main street past the triangle and on towards the narrow bridge across the river at the end of the town.

"Sure, half the place is boarded up and for sale. I don't know what happened to it. I used to enjoy coming out to Sweeney's Hotel here for a meal or a quiet pint, but even that's closed now. It's a shame," Hays said.

Galway FM Radio was blasting out the usual mix of tired Christmas songs, punctuated by advertising from the various gift shops in the city, imploring last minute shoppers to get their loved ones something precious and expensive to mark the occasion. Lyons turned the radio off almost immediately.

"So, what's the plan out here?" she said.

"We'll have to play it by ear. Let's see what the manager can tell us about their arrangements for their takings, and give us an idea of the sums they will be handling the day after St Stephen's Day. When we have that, we'll be able to decide what best to do. Do you think the Geraghtys would really go for it after what happened with the postman?" Hays said.

"Well, something is keeping them out here in the wild west, and it isn't the weather. And I think they know that when they are caught they'll be going down for a long time, so they probably want to get as much cash together as they can for their families for when they're away."

"Yeah, you're probably right. I've known a good few criminals playing that game," Hays said.

"Or, it could just be that they're waiting for Christmas day to make their escape, thinking that there'll be none of us around. Who knows. But we can't afford to take any chances," Lyons said.

Chapter Eighteen

The two detectives called in on Séan Mulholland as a courtesy before they reached the Abbey Glen.

"Ah, 'tis yourselves," Mulholland said with a big welcoming smile.

"I hope you've brought my Christmas present? And there I was thinking you'd forgotten all about us out here in Clifden."

They exchanged seasonal greetings, and then Mulholland offered them coffee, which they gladly accepted. They needed refreshment after the drive.

As Séan Mulholland put their two mugs of instant coffee down on the table, he asked, "Would you like a little drop in that to warm you up, given it's the festive season?"

"Ah no, you're grand Séan," said Lyons, answering for both of them.

"So, tell us, this man Wallace out at the Abbey Glen, what's he like?" Hays asked.

"He seems like a decent sort of a chap, for an Englishman. He's been manager out there for about three years now, and he always treats us fairly. He's nice enough too," Mulholland said.

From what Mulholland had said, it seemed Mr Wallace had realised that a certain amount of generosity towards the local Gardaí was tactically a good idea, and while it hardly amounted to bribery, he felt sure that Séan and perhaps some of the others based in Clifden, had benefitted from the hotel's hospitality from time to time.

"Well, at least the man isn't stupid," Hays thought to himself.

As they drank their coffee, Lyons shared their theory about the possibility of the Geraghtys hijacking the Christmas takings.

"God, Maureen, that could get very messy. Do you think they'd be that audacious?" Mulholland said.

"I do, to be honest. They've shown no fear so far, and if they'd kill a postman in more or less cold blood, and shoot a Garda, then they're a pretty bad lot," she said.

"Mmm, I see what you mean. OK, well why don't you go on out to see Wallace and let me know what he thinks? You can rely on our help here in any case, whatever's going down. The lads want to see those two put away for a very long time. Paddy McKeever was well liked in this place," Mulholland said.

"Thanks, Séan. We'll let you know, though I've a feeling we'll be getting the heavy mob out again if there's a chance the Geraghtys will be mounting a raid. But the more men we can get out the better," Hays said.

"Oh, and by the way, Séan, Pascal Brosnan still has my sidearm," Lyons said.

"Yes, I know. He was on to me about it. I told him to keep it till he can return it to you personally. It's OK, he

120

has a gun safe at his house. He has his own twelve bore that he uses to shoot rabbits out on the headland at Dog's Bay," Mulholland said.

"That's fine. Maybe I'll leave it with him till this lot is over," Lyons said.

* * *

The Abbey Glen Hotel is situated down a private driveway off the Sky Road, on the far side of Clifden from the Garda Station. It's built in the form of an old castle, and prides itself on being the finest lodgings available in the area. The hotel has an interesting history, having been originally constructed in the mid-nineteenth century. It started out as a family home, but later became an orphanage, and for a time was operated as the Glenowen Hotel, before being bought by the current owners in 1969, and then refurbished to a very high standard, and getting a new name.

When Hays and Lyons arrived at the hotel, it was quite busy, and they waited at reception for several minutes before being greeted by a male receptionist with a name badge identifying him as Edward.

"Good morning, sir, madam. How may I help you today?" Edward said.

Hays produced his warrant card and said, "We'd like to see Mr Wallace if he's available please."

"Certainly, Inspector. I'll page him for you now. I think he's in the banqueting suite getting things ready for Christmas dinner," the young man said.

Edward used a small, discreet, walkie-talkie to contact the manager, and a few minutes later, a man wearing impeccable white shirt, black jacket and striped trousers approached.

"Good morning, Inspector," Wallace said, extending his hand to Hays. Hays shook his hand noting that Wallace had a good firm grip, and introduced Lyons.

Lionel Wallace was only about five foot nine in stature, yet he exuded the presence and confidence of a man much taller than that. This was a man well used to asserting himself, and Hays felt certain that he managed the establishment with a combination of charm and fear.

"Mr Wallace, I wonder if you could spare us a few minutes in your office. It's rather delicate I'm afraid," Hays said.

"Yes, of course, certainly," the man said, ushering them down a corridor with his right arm extended. Lyons noticed that he gestured to Edward as they departed, and Edward must have understood the signal, for he nodded almost imperceptibly in response.

Wallace's office was in keeping with the splendour of the rest of the place, with an antique desk and Chippendale styled dining chairs with genuine ceramic casters placed appropriately in front of it. Wallace's own chair was of the captain's variety, and Lyons didn't miss the symbolism.

Wallace gestured for the two detectives to be seated, and almost as soon as they were, a knock on the door announced the arrival of a tray bearing a silver coffee pot, cups and saucers and a plate of delicious looking pastries, as well as a bowl of mixed brown and white lump sugar.

Wallace poured out the three cups of coffee, and offered cream and sugar, before asking, "Now then, folks, what can I do for you?"

Lyons explained their theory that there might be an attempt to rob the hotel of its takings on the day after St

Stephen's Day, and asked the manager about the arrangements for making the lodgement.

"It's quite simple really. I take the money in my car into town and deposit it at the bank. There has never been any trouble. It's very quiet around here at ten in the morning," Wallace said.

"And how much cash would you expect to have in that lodgement, Mr Wallace?" Hays said.

"Well, it's hard to be accurate, but last year if I remember correctly it was about twenty-two thousand in cash. I know it seems a lot, but most of our bar takings are in cash, and a lot of the ticket sales for the Stephen's Night party come in cash too, so it soon builds up. But we have a very secure safe here on the premises. The room it's in is alarmed, and there's CCTV on the safe itself at all times."

"Who goes with you to the bank, Mr Wallace?" Lyons asked.

"No one. I go on my own. Everyone is very busy cleaning up after the party, so I don't like to interrupt their work. But it's not a problem."

"Well, Mr Wallace, we believe that it is possible that an attempt may be made to rob you on the way to the bank with the takings. We can't be sure of course, that's the pity of it, but we have received information that leads us to believe there may be something planned," Hays said.

"So," he went on, "we'd like to change the arrangements if that's OK with you?"

"I see. What do you have in mind?"

Hays went on to outline their plan for the morning after the party, and while Wallace didn't seem to be entirely comfortable with it, once he heard that the robbers could be armed and had already shown no reluctance to use their weapons, he warmed to their idea.

"Tell you what," Wallace said, becoming more cheerful again, "why don't you two come to our party? You can stay over if you like – I'm sure we can find you a couple of rooms for the night, and then you'll be on site as it were for the following morning. No charge of course."

"That's very generous of you, Mr Wallace, but much as we would like to, we will have other things to arrange in advance, so we had better take a rain check. Perhaps some other time?" Lyons said.

"Yes, of course, silly of me. And of course, we will arrange for you to stay on another occasion."

Chapter Nineteen

On Christmas Day Hays stayed in bed later than Maureen, claiming that his leg was sore and he needed to rest. Lyons was happy with the arrangement, as it gave her a chance to wrap his present, and write a card which she delicately attached to the package with a yellow silk ribbon.

Lyons had managed to sneak out to Purcell Marine in Clarinbridge to buy Hays' Musto jacket. The lady in the shop had assured Lyons that if it wasn't the right size, she could bring it back and change it, or even get a refund if it wasn't to his liking, but she assured Lyons that it was the best possible quality, and even knocked a few euro off the price. Lyons hoped he would be pleased with it.

Hays wasn't just pleased, he was delighted.

"God, Maureen, how the hell did you manage that? I never suspected a thing!"

"Sleight of hand and classic distraction techniques, love. But I'm glad you didn't spot it. The woman in Purcell's said I could change it if it doesn't fit, but unless you've put on a stone or two in hospital, it should be just right."

"And now I feel awful. I haven't managed to get you anything. I'm sorry," he said putting his arm around her.

"Don't be daft. I wasn't expecting anything with you being in hospital and all. We can sort it out after. It'll just cost you double!" she said, laughing and giving him a slow kiss.

"Would you fancy a run out to Sheila's after lunch? They're very keen we should put in an appearance if at all possible, though if you're not up to it, I'm sure they'll understand," Lyons said.

"OK. Let's see what we feel like after dinner – I presume we are having a Christmas dinner?" Hays said, slightly worried.

"Yep. I'll be putting on the spaghetti hoops in about half an hour. Hope you're hungry," she teased.

"That doesn't smell like spaghetti hoops to me, Lyons. It smells like a Maureen special, and yes, I'm bloody starving!"

With Hays' leg still in bandages, they had to forego their usual brisk Christmas morning walk along the promenade in Salthill, where a group of unusually hardy swimmers gathered for a short dunk in the freezing water.

While Lyons attended to the meal, Hays watched tv, but wasn't really engaged with what was being shown. His mind was turning over various scenarios about the potential heist the day after tomorrow, and how best they might deal with it, if indeed, it was to happen at all.

At one thirty Lyons called through to the lounge to say that dinner was ready, and Hays went back to the kitchen-diner to find a magnificent spread. The table was decorated in all sorts of Christmas paraphernalia, and Lyons had made a fruit cocktail starter involving grapefruit, oranges and a copious amount of sweet sherry.

She had roasted a capon along with all the usual accompaniments for the main course. The bird had been chosen for its relatively manageable size, there being only the two of them, and it was cooked to perfection with crispy brown skin and delicious stuffing.

"What do you think about going out to Sheila's? We needn't stay long," she said as they progressed through the meal.

"Yeah, sure. Have you told her we're coming?" Hays said.

"Not specifically. I wasn't sure if you'd be up for it. But I said we'd try and make it out for a while if we could. I have presents for the kids that I'd like to unload."

* * *

Sheila Burke, as she now was, lived on what had been the family farm in a townland known as Cartymore. There were no boys in the Lyons family, and it was clear from quite early on that Maureen wasn't likely to want to run the farm as her father got older and less able to manage.

Sheila had shown more of an interest, and when she started going out with Séamus, whom she married at twenty-two, the deal was sealed. Séamus and Sheila would run the farm, which by this time ran to almost a hundred acres of mixed arable and grazing land, but Maureen would retain a one third ownership of the property and land as a sort of sleeping partner. So far, the arrangement had worked well. When the farm became essentially dissected by the new M17 motorway, albeit with an underpass to allow Séamus to move livestock and machinery between the two unequal halves of the land, compensation had been paid by the council. Sheila had offered to split it with Maureen, but after a bit of haggling, it was agreed that the money should be used to improve the farmhouse, which had been built in the 1920s and hadn't seen much refurbishment in old man Lyons' day.

The result was a completely modernised dwelling, with a large open plan kitchen diner with new fitted units and a gorgeous AGA range. This had been accomplished by building an extension to the west side of the house, and an additional two bedrooms, with a very large master suite that included a sizeable walk-in wardrobe and a lovely en-suite shower room fully tiled, with underfloor heating. The house hadn't consumed all of the compensation money, for Séamus was canny with it, and appeared to have obtained remarkable value for the work needed on the house, so after a further family pow-wow, the balance was spent erecting a purpose built steel and concrete shed to accommodate the valuable farm machinery. When it was completed, Maureen got an officer from the Galway crime prevention unit out to advise on how best to secure Séamus' machinery, and the building now had a very fancy alarm system, and a number of well-concealed CCTV cameras, all rigged up to send a message to Séamus' phone, in the event of any disturbance around the farm. The security arrangements were completed by the ever present 'Lucky', a very even-tempered German Shepherd dog, who barked like a thing possessed and bared a serious mouthful of sharp white teeth if anyone came near the farmyard.

Séamus also held a licensed shotgun, and he had said many times that he would have no hesitation in using it to defend his property and his family should the occasion arise. Theft of expensive tractors and other farm machinery had become a small industry in recent times around Galway, and often the perpetrators would steal the equipment at around 2 a.m., and have it on the 6:30 ferry out to England before the farmer was even aware that it had gone. Maureen had told him that he was entitled to defend himself, his family, and his property, but that he should be careful how he went about it. If a robber was coming at him with a weapon, then he would probably be OK if he shot him in the legs, but that under no circumstances should he shoot anyone in the back who could be said to be retreating. Previous case law had made it clear on these points.

Séamus responded by saying, "I'll make sure the bugger has a weapon all right, but you know how it is with a shotgun, it's not that accurate and if it was dark, he might just end up with a few pellets in his groin or his gut!"

Maureen assured Séamus that she knew all about shotgun wounds, and what they could do to a person.

The drive out to Cartymore was pleasant enough. There were some broken clouds in the sky, with the low winter sun breaking through from time to time, casting long shadows on the landscape. It was surprisingly warm too, at nine degrees according to the outside temperature gauge on Hays' Mercedes, but he knew that by nightfall, especially if it remained relatively clear, the temperature would probably fall to near freezing. Traffic was extremely light, and they covered the twenty-eight kilometres in just over half an hour.

When they arrived at the Burke house, Lucky came out to greet them in his usual manner, but immediately softened when he realised it was Maureen, who petted his head affectionately, and was rewarded with enthusiastic licking of her extended hand.

They struggled into the house armed with what seemed to Hays to be a serious load of nicely wrapped gifts that Maureen had purchased in the weeks leading up to the holiday, whenever she got a chance.

Sheila and Séamus had four kids. There were two boys and two girls, the boys being the elder at eleven and nine, and the two girls at seven and six. The house was quite chaotic, with discarded wrapping paper taking up a lot of floor space, and the two boys darting around, one with an enormous fire engine, and the other with a model JCB that looked as if it could be capable of even more than the real thing, with motorised arms and buckets to the front and rear, and working lights.

Sheila and Maureen sat down over a pot of tea to catch up, while Séamus and Mick retired to the peace of the front room. Mick was of course offered a drink, but declined, as he was driving.

"I hear you've been in the wars, Mick," Séamus said when they were seated.

"Yes. Some buggers took a pot shot at me out in Roundstone after that postman was killed."

"I heard about that, OK. Nasty business. Did you catch them?"

"Not yet. But I'm hopeful. I can't say too much, but the next day or two will be crucial," Hays said.

"The Geraghty brothers, I heard," said Séamus.

"We think so, yes, in fact, it is them. What have you heard?" Hays said.

"There's an old guy down at the pub at the crossroads most nights that seems to have some knowledge of their activities. I think there may be a family connection, but I don't say anything, I just listen."

"Have you heard anything specific?" Hays said.

"No, but I'd say he's probably down there now, if you want to take a wander?"

"What? On Christmas day! Surely the place is closed."

"Well of course it is, but there'll still be a few of the locals in around now, just to get away from the family, having a couple of pints. Harmless enough," Séamus said.

"Might be worth a look. Can you get in?"

"Of course. I know the owner pretty well. We've done a bit of business from time to time," Séamus said.

Hays didn't dare enquire as to the nature of the business – he was sure it wasn't too ethical.

Séamus read his mind.

"Ah, nothing heavy, you understand. My brother works for the brewery, and I can slip him the odd keg of lager now and then, and he returns the favour with the occasional bottle of whiskey. Just a kind of barter arrangement. Then he keeps me informed about any strangers in the area that might be thinking of nicking stuff, that sort of thing."

"OK," said Hays, "let's take a stroll down to the crossroads then. I'll tell the girls," Hays said.

"Ah, don't bother Mick. We'll slip out the front. They'll figure it out if they need to."

Chapter Twenty

The pub at the crossroads had no name over the door. It was an austere grey building clad in sand and cement plaster, with what might have been a shop window once, facing out to the road, with a wooden surround painted in a dreary sort of dark wine colour. Dirty net curtains hung in the window to prevent prying eyes from seeing in.

Séamus and Mick went around the back of the building where weeds were growing up through the broken concrete paths. Séamus knocked twice, and then three times in quick succession on the back door with its peeling paint and slowly rotting architraves, and a moment later the door opened an inch or two.

"Ah, Séamus, come in. There's just a few of us having a quiet drink given the occasion," said Dónal, who was clearly the owner of the establishment.

"Thanks, Dónal, this is Mick, my brother-in-law. He's from Galway," Séamus said, as if that would excuse any odd behaviour the inspector might portray.

Inside, the place was dark, with just a couple of low wattage light bulbs hanging down over the wooden bar. A selection of stools stood along the length of it that had seen better days, with three old guys in dirty grey suits perched on them, each with a pint of Guinness and a glass of whiskey in front of them.

Séamus asked for a pint for each of them, and left ten euro on the counter.

The nearest old man nodded at Mick, and said, "Grand weather for it, don't ye think?"

"It is indeed. Let's hope the rain holds off for the rest of the day," Hays replied.

"What is it you do then?" the man went on.

"I work for the post office in Galway," Hays lied.

"Oh, right. God, it was a terrible thing that happened to that poor man out in Roundstone."

"Yes, it was, poor Paddy. He left a widow you know. Very sad," Hays said.

"I don't suppose the Gardaí are anywhere near to catching the bastards that did it," the old man said.

"I don't know. They're in and out a bit to us, but they don't say much," Hays said.

"I'd say those fellas could go again, you know. Do another one before they're caught."

"Surely not. They got quite a good bit of cash from poor Paddy's van. That'll probably do them," Hays said.

"Well, maybe, but I hear different. They're still out there you know. Now why's that? I wouldn't like to be carrying a lot of cash around with those two on the loose," the old man said, taking a generous swig of his pint.

"Yes, but what sort of place would have a lot of cash just now?" Hays said. He realised he was pushing it a bit, but he'd only get one chance at this if the old guy did know something.

"Ah, ye know, some of them fancy hotels and the like." He drained his pint glass, and followed up with a good mouthful of the whiskey.

"Can I get you another?" Hays asked.

"No, you're all right. You can't buy your way into good company." And with that, the old guy slipped down from his perch, and headed out the back door.

Hays and Séamus spent a little while longer chatting to Dónal and his odd mix of clients. Then they made their excuses, saying that the women would be hopping mad if they stayed too long, thanked Dónal for his hospitality, and slipped quietly back out into the fading afternoon light.

* * *

Back at the farm, Sheila had laid out tea. There was an enormous homemade Christmas cake and mince pies with loads of cream. She insisted that Maureen and Mick had some of both "for the journey back", as if it was a lot more than half an hour in the car, but they didn't like to offend so they managed a piece of cake and a mince pie each, and then departed with Lyons clutching a small collection of nicely wrapped gifts for them both from Sheila and her husband.

On the way back in the car, Lyons quizzed Hays about where he had disappeared to with Séamus during the afternoon.

Hays told her about the shebeen that they had visited and outlined the conversation that had taken place down at the old pub.

"Crikey, Mick. It's a good job you weren't caught in there by some of the boys from Athenry," Lyons said.

"I'm sure they're well aware, Maureen. They'll probably be along later themselves for a few drinks. There's a different way of doing things out here in the country. Anyway, the old geezer definitely knew something, but of course he was being careful not to give too much away. I got the feeling that there was some connection between him and the Geraghtys. Let's check to see if there are any other "fancy hotels" open out that way. I wouldn't like to end up in the wrong place again. Can you look after that while I set up the welcoming committee for our two heroes when we get into the office tomorrow?" Hays said.

When they got back home, Lyons put calls through to the other up-market hotels out near Clifden. The Lahinch Castle was obviously closed, with a pre-recorded message advising callers that the hotel would re-open on January 4th, and giving a phone number for a security company in the event of an emergency. At the Renvyle House, the phone was answered.

"Oh, hello. Can I ask if the hotel is open at the moment?" Lyons asked.

"I'm sorry, no. We're closed till January. We have a small private party here for today and tomorrow, and then we're closed till the first weekend in January," the girl said.

"Oh, right, thanks. Sorry to disturb you," Lyons said, finishing the call.

Just in case, she tried the Alcock and Brown and Foyle's in Clifden itself, and ascertained that they too were closed for the holiday, so it looked as if the Abbey Glen was the only establishment functioning normally in the area over the holiday.

Chapter Twenty-one

They rose at nine o'clock on St Stephen's day, and had a hearty breakfast. Then they decided to go into Mill Street where they would have more resources at their disposal, although there would probably be only a few Gardaí around, given the day.

There was a strange, almost ghostly, atmosphere in the station, and a stillness that neither of them were used to.

Hays broke the silence with a call to the superintendent at home. He outlined their plan for the following day, and asked if the Super could line up support from the Armed Response Unit.

"God, Mick, I don't know. They're still smarting after being called out to Clifden for no good reason. How sure are you about this?" Plunkett asked.

"To be very honest, not sure at all, sir. But that doesn't mean we shouldn't follow it up. We will look very stupid indeed if there is a robbery and we're nowhere near it, or worse still, we're there, ill-equipped, and as a result officers come to harm," Hays said.

"I see what you mean. OK, leave it with me. I get on fairly well with the man at the top of that outfit, I'll see what I can do. If I get lucky, can you provide a briefing this afternoon?"

"Yes, of course, sir, no problem. Thanks, sir," Hays said.

"Don't thank me yet, Mick. I'll get back to you."

While Hays was dealing with Plunkett, Lyons had busied herself with the Ordnance Survey map of the area around the Abbey Glen Hotel, and had looked up Google Earth, printing off some very good images of the hotel, the driveway down to it from the Sky Road, and other features of the immediate vicinity.

"This is a picture of the hotel and the avenue down to it from the road," she said, pointing to the printout when Hays came back into the room.

"I reckon they'll spring their trap after the manager has come up the drive and turned the bend, just before the cattle grid and the exit onto the road. There will be less chance of being seen in case there is someone passing by, and there's room to park a vehicle in at the side just there too," Lyons said.

"Hmm, that makes sense, I guess. So where do you think we should position ourselves?" Hays said.

"Well, you'll presumably be driving the manager's car. I can hide in the back of his car, and we should see how many ARU officers they allocate, but I reckon we'll need at least two further up the drive, hidden down behind the hedge. That will give us maximum cover for whatever goes down. What time do you want to get out there at?" she said.

"The bank opens at ten, and the manager said he usually leaves the hotel at about five to, but the Geraghtys may be observing from a good bit earlier, so I'd say we need to be there about seven thirty. Would you agree?" Hays said.

"Sounds about right. Do we want to get Seán to provide any local backup?"

"I thought about that, and I'd say no. We don't want the area bristling with police – that will just frighten them off; or give them more targets to shoot at!"

Superintendent Plunkett called Hays back just before lunch.

"Right, Mick. The best they'll do is two armed officers. They'll be with you at three o'clock for a briefing, and will be at your disposal from early morning tomorrow till whenever this thing is over. Is that all right?" the senior officer said.

"Thanks, sir, that will do nicely. It's a pretty confined area, so two men should be able to cover it handily enough. And Maureen and myself will be armed as well. Thanks for your help, sir," Hays said.

"No bother, Mick. But do one thing for me now," Plunkett said.

"What's that, sir?"

"Don't mess it up!"

When Hays hung up, Lyons said, "Only one of us will be armed. Remember, Pascal Brosnan has my pistol."

"That's OK. You can have mine, I'll be driving," Hays said.

While they were waiting for the ARU officers to arrive, Lyons telephoned the manager out at the Abbey Glen and outlined their plan to him.

"We'll take your car with the lodgement in the boot at about nine fifty-five. Senior Inspector Hays will drive, and I'll be concealed in the rear of the car. There will be other support units in place as well. If nothing happens, you follow us into Clifden about ten minutes behind to complete the lodgement at the bank. But stay put until you get the all clear from us. Is that OK, Mr Wallace?" she said.

"Yes, I suppose so. Do you really think there will be an attempt made? With guns?"

"It's certainly a possibility, Mr Wallace, so we don't want to take any chances. See you tomorrow bright and early."

* * *

Just before three o'clock in the afternoon, the two ARU Gardaí arrived into Mill Street. They were young men, in their late twenties, Maureen gauged; thin, wiry, and a bit mean looking, their appearance being somewhat exaggerated by their extremely scruffy attire.

Tom and Ronan were their names, but they would be referred to as T1 and R1 during the operation itself. It was important for ARU officers to remain entirely anonymous whilst on operational duties.

Hays and Lyons briefed the two men on the situation, and their plan to lure the Geraghtys to the hotel with the promise of a sizeable cash haul from the Christmas takings.

Tom was the first to speak after the plan had been outlined.

"Is there somewhere we can put our jeep out of the way?" he said.

"Yes, there is. There's an empty house about two hundred metres further along the Sky Road with an empty shed beside it that has gates that close over. You can park it in there well out of sight," Hays said.

"What do you think of the plan?" Hays asked.

"It's very dangerous. It's very likely that there will be an exchange of fire between some of us and the Geraghtys, and that could go one way or the other. It's high risk, and I don't like the fact that you will be driving the manager's car, I don't like it at all," Tom said.

"That's why we asked for you guys," Hays said.

"Well, we'll do our best, but there are no guarantees once people start shooting. In our experience, anything can happen, and usually does. Isn't that right, Ronan?" Tom said.

"Yeah, but it looks to me as if someone has to put a stop to these two. Might as well be us," Ronan said almost casually.

"How will we know you're in position?" Lyons asked.

"You won't. We can't afford to use the radios in advance of the gig. But don't worry, we'll be there."

For another hour, the small group discussed various scenarios in case things went wrong. They formed three different plans covering all the likely scenarios that they could envisage.

At five o'clock, Tom and Ronan departed, leaving Hays and Lyons to contemplate the day ahead with some trepidation.

"God, Maureen, I hope this doesn't come unstuck. It could end very badly," Hays said on the way home in the car.

"You and me both, sunshine, you and me both," she said.

They spent the rest of the evening having a quiet meal at home, although neither of them had a strong appetite. They didn't have a drink. They wanted to ensure that they would both have clear heads in the morning.

They went to bed at ten, setting their alarm for 06:00, and fell into a restless sleep.

Chapter Twenty-two

It was a dark wet morning in Galway when Hays and Lyons were awoken by their alarm clock. It was also very early.

They moved around each other silently as they washed and dressed in warm winter clothes, and were ready to leave their house in Salthill by soon after six thirty.

The temperature gauge on Hays' Mercedes indicated that it was just four degrees outside, but with the dampness from the rain, it felt more like freezing. As the heater in the car started to warm them, they discussed the operation ahead.

"Are you nervous?" Lyons asked her partner as they cleared the city, totally bereft of any vestige of traffic so early on this holiday morning.

"Apprehensive would be more accurate, Maureen. We don't know exactly what we're getting into out here, and I don't feel we have nearly enough cover, so maybe I should be a little nervous. What about you?" Hays said.

"I'm just plain nervous, Mick. Still, it will sharpen our senses and keep the adrenalin flowing. Are you happy with the plan?"

"More or less. I think it's the best we can do given the information we have been given. But there's something else," Hays said.

"What's that?"

"I'm feeling that I can't guarantee your safety as things stand, and that bothers the hell out of me," Hays said.

"Look, Mick. I know what we both signed up for with this job. I knew it wasn't all going to be pick-pockets and bicycle thieves we'd be dealing with. But if we can stay professional and detached, and relax in the knowledge that both of us know how to look after ourselves, then we'll come out of it all right, or at least we'll give ourselves the best chance."

"Hmm, you're right, of course. But I have an uneasy feeling about today, that's all."

They drove on out in a westerly direction. The pelting rain and heavy accompanying cloud cover meant that the inky darkness enveloped their car, and at times Hays had to slow down to see where he was going. They couldn't afford to go off the road at this juncture.

Lyons couldn't help thinking of the contrast between this drive and the many journeys she had made in glorious sunshine out over this same road, when the blue of the distant mountains, and the bright yellow of the gorse in full bloom created a picture postcard view.

They reached the Abbey Glen just after eight o'clock. It was still almost pitch dark, but the hotel was bathed in floodlighting making it stand out from the surrounding gloom.

Inside, Lionel Wallace was busy overseeing the clear up from the party the previous night, which, by all accounts, had been a resounding success.

"Good morning, folks. What a dreadful day. Did you have a good drive out?" the manager asked.

"Good morning, Mr Wallace. Yes, it was OK. How are things here?" Lyons said.

"We're just getting to grips with the clean-up. We had a huge crowd in last night. I suspect most of the guests are hungover. Would you like some breakfast?"

"Yes, thank you, that would be great," Hays said, and Wallace led the way into the morning room where a few tables were set with white cloths and all the trappings of a four-star breakfast.

Wallace gestured to a table by the window that looked out over the harbour to Clifden Bay.

"Please, order whatever you like, and it's on me," he said before quickly busying himself elsewhere.

They ordered a hearty breakfast with lots of strong coffee.

Outside, although it was still almost pitch dark, they could just about make out the few boats that were bobbing about in the harbour, and the open sea beyond, the waves topped with white horses whipped up by the prevailing on-shore wind.

With breakfast over, they sought out Lionel Wallace again, and went with him to his office. There, he opened the hotel's safe, and withdrew what seemed like a very large amount of cash, all neatly bundled up in fifty, twenty, ten, and five euro bundles, wrapped in plastic, with a sticker from the hotel fixed to each one so that the bank would know where the money had come from.

"There's just short of twenty-seven thousand here," Wallace said soberly, putting the bundles into a leather bag and snapping it closed.

"Over to you now, Inspector," Wallace said, handing the bag to Hays somewhat reluctantly as if he might never see the money again.

"Thanks, Mr Wallace. And may we have your car keys please? It's the black Audi parked out front, is that right?"

"Yes, that's the one," he said, handing over a single key. As the two detectives turned to leave the room, Wallace said, "Oh, Inspector – good luck!"

Hays took the bag outside and placed it in the boot of the manager's car. He then retrieved his Sig Sauer P220 from the compartment in the boot of his own Mercedes and gave it to Lyons.

"It's loaded and primed, Maureen, but the safety is on. Let's hope you don't have to use it."

As had been agreed, Maureen Lyons got into the back of the car and made herself invisible by hunkering down in the back seat. Hays sat into the driver's position, started the car and pointed it up along the driveway leading to the Sky Road. He moved off.

As Hays rounded the bend in the driveway, he was met by Anselm Geraghty standing in the middle of the track, a sawn-off shotgun in his right hand braced against his hip. Hays recognized the scruffy young man with the greasy fair hair from Deasy's description. With his left hand, Geraghty signalled Hays to stop. There was no point in Hays accelerating in an attempt to run the thief over – it would just have ended in the same way as the poor postman, and that would have served no one well.

Hays brought the car to a halt, saying to Lyons, "Here we go. Get ready for some fireworks!"

Lyons thought about getting out of the car's back door, but she felt certain that such a move could prompt Geraghty to use his weapon, and in any case, she had no idea where the other brother was. Nor was there any point, she thought, in attempting to shoot Geraghty through the windscreen. She would probably miss, and it wouldn't end well. For the moment, there was nothing she could do except wait.

Geraghty signalled Hays to get out of the car.

Hays opened the door, and stepped out, feeling a distinct twinge in his thigh from the last time this thug had shot him. He tried to use the car door as a shield, but Geraghty told him to stand clear, and with a loaded gun pointed at him, he wasn't about to argue.

As Hays emerged from the cover of the car, Geraghty raised the shotgun to his shoulder and shouted at Hays, "This is for Joey."

Lyons watched helplessly as she was sure she was about to see her partner gunned down in cold blood.

As Geraghty started to tighten his finger around the trigger of the shotgun, a single shot rang out, shattering the early morning peace like a thunderbolt.

Geraghty's body convulsed as a red mist spread out from his shoulder. His gun went up in the air and both barrels discharged harmlessly into the brightening sky. He fell with a clatter to the ground, yelping in pain, his right hand now cradling his bloody shoulder.

T1 stepped out of the hedgerow where he had been concealed, and walked over to the prone form of Anselm Geraghty writhing on the ground. He pointed his M4 carbine at the man's head, and told him not to move.

"Thanks, Tom. Nice one," Hays said to the ARU officer.

"You're welcome, sir, it's what we do," he said coolly.

Just as they were all calming down, the younger Geraghty ran from behind them and crossed the hedge into the adjacent field, emerging a few metres further up onto the driveway and hopping into a blue Peugeot that had been parked at the side of the avenue close to the main road.

The engine in the little car roared as it took off, but not before R1 had fired a single shot in through the back window of the car. His bullet, though, failed to hit the target, and the Peugeot accelerated away swerving left and right, with its tyres squealing, towards Clifden.

Lyons, who had been on the phone calling an ambulance for the beleaguered older brother, finished the call quickly, and redialled Clifden Garda station.

"Séan, it's Maureen. We have a blue Peugeot 208 registration number 02 G 96202 heading your way with an armed and dangerous criminal inside. Can you get some road blocks organised quickly, and get the other stations in the area to do the same? We need to box this guy in before he gets away again."

"God, righto Maureen. Is everyone OK?" Mulholland said.

"I'll fill you in later. There's no time to waste."

Lyons finally got a chance to talk to her partner.

"Jesus, Mick, that looked pretty bad for a few moments there. Are you OK?" Lyons said taking his hand briefly.

"I'm fine. But do you know what was going through my mind as I faced the little toe-rag?"

"Go on," she said, thinking this should be good.

"I haven't made a will. If he shot me as he intended, you'd get nothing – not the house, my boat, my paltry pension – nothing," Hays said.

"Ah, away with ye, Mick Hays, sure what would I be doing with all that junk anyway?" She squeezed his hand a little more tightly.

As they stood around waiting for the ambulance to arrive, Hays' phone started to ring.

"Inspector, this is Lionel Wallace. We heard shots. Is everything OK?"

"That depends on who you ask. We're all OK thanks, but there's a thief here lying on the ground that has been wounded, and he's definitely not OK. The ambulance is on its way," Hays said.

"Oh, gosh. And dare I ask about the lodgement?"

"Safe and sound, Mr Wallace, safe and sound."

"Do you think the driveway could be cleared soon? Some of our guests are keen to get underway. Understandable, I suppose," Wallace said.

"It will be another hour or so before we can let any cars up or down. Is there no other way out of the hotel?" Hays said.

"There's a footpath that goes down to the harbour, but these people have cars."

"I suggest you offer them some complimentary refreshments and explain the situation to them. I'm sure they'll be understanding. We'll get the access clear as soon as we can, and I'll let you know when you can come and take your car and the lodgement into Clifden."

* * *

When Hays had finished the call with the hotel manager, he could hear the wail of an ambulance approaching. When it came to a halt at the entrance to the hotel, two paramedics jumped out and trotted over to where Anselm Geraghty lay on the ground.

Lyons recognised the female paramedic from previous encounters.

"Morning, Jean," she said, watching the girl getting to work on the injured man.

"Oh hi, Inspector. What happened here then?"

Lyons explained the circumstances of the shooting to the paramedic, although it was hardly necessary as Tom was still standing over Geraghty pointing his gun at his head.

"Could you put that thing away please, officer, before someone else gets shot?" Jean said edgily.

"If you're happy that he no longer represents a threat," Tom replied.

"Look at him. What do you think?" Jean said.

"Hmmm, OK. Will he live?" Tom said.

"If you'd clear off and let me get on with my job here, then yes, probably."

Jean didn't like guns. She had seen first-hand the damage they could do to a body, and this was just another instance as far as she was concerned.

Chapter Twenty-three

Emmet Geraghty drove the small blue Peugeot like a man possessed. Although he was a tough young criminal, seeing his elder brother gunned down in front of him was something he never expected. He didn't know if Anselm was dead or alive, but either way, he wouldn't be seeing him for some time to come.

Emmet still had most of the proceeds of the post office van robbery in the boot of the Peugeot, now liberally sprinkled with broken glass thanks to the ARU officer who had fired at him.

The car was pretty useless anyway, and he'd have to swap it soon before it gave up the ghost entirely. He knew exactly where to go.

Tadgh Deasy had his head under the bonnet of an old Nissan Primera when the blue Peugeot came skidding into the yard and slid to a halt on the oily concrete. Geraghty jumped out and looked at Deasy who had by now straightened up and was staring curiously at the state of the car that Geraghty had arrived in.

Before Deasy could open his mouth, the agitated Geraghty shouted across the yard, "I need a new car, and I need it now!"

Deasy didn't like the look of this at all. He had already been in trouble with the local Gardaí for supplying this lot with the Pajero, and he had been stripped of the proceeds of the transaction in any case.

"Sorry, mate. You're out of luck. I have nothing here that goes at the minute," Deasy said, and he turned to go back to work on the ageing Primera.

Geraghty returned to the Peugeot, retrieving something from the back seat, and walked back over to where Deasy was working.

"Is that so?" Geraghty said, pointing the business end of another sawn-off shotgun at Deasy's temple.

Shay Deasy, Tadgh's son, was in his bedroom, and heard the commotion in the yard below. He looked out to see his father being held at gunpoint by Emmet Geraghty. He wasted no time in calling Pascal Brosnan in Roundstone Garda station.

When Brosnan got the call, he knew exactly what to do. He locked up the little Garda station, leaving the usual note pinned to the front door. "Station unattended at present. In an emergency, contact Clifden Garda station." Numbers were listed to allow for that eventuality.

At his home, which was just a few hundred metres from the station, Brosnan took the gun that Maureen Lyons had lent him out of his gun safe. He primed the chamber and set the safety catch, tucked the loaded gun down the front of his jacket, and then set off as fast as he dared towards Deasy's yard, which was only a couple of kilometres on the Recess side of the village. It took him no more than four minutes to cover the distance.

* * *

"OK, OK, Jesus, take it easy. I'll get you something, but it will take me a few minutes to make sure it has fuel and is good for the road," Deasy said.

Geraghty seemed to calm down a little, but still kept the gun trained on Tadgh Deasy as he went about selecting a vehicle from his seedy stock to give to the young man.

As Tadgh Deasy was unlocking a rather tired looking Ford Focus with an 05 plate, Brosnan's multicoloured squad car drove briskly into the yard, its blue lights illuminating the dreary, overcast sky. At exactly the same moment, Shay Deasy opened the back door of the house looking out onto the yard and shouted, "Hey, you, leave my dad alone!"

Geraghty didn't know which way to turn. In the confusion, he aimed the shotgun at Shay who was now standing about twenty metres away, a likely fatal distance if the gun was discharged.

Brosnan was out of his car with the driver's window rolled down, and using the car's door for protection, he took careful aim and fired a single shot from Lyons' gun.

His aim was good. The bullet entered Emmet Geraghty's right knee cap, shattering the bone, and causing its owner to crumple quickly to the ground. He dropped the shotgun as he fell, and it clattered harmlessly away.

Geraghty was rolling in agony on the dirty yard floor, shouting obscenities at the Garda who had brought him down, but Brosnan didn't care. He carefully removed the magazine from his gun, and emptied the chamber, before placing it back in the boot of the squad car, and locking it.

Then, putting on vinyl gloves, he retrieved the shotgun, breaking it, and removed the two twelve bore cartridges, placing them in an evidence bag.

With the scene secured, he called his sergeant in Clifden.

"Sergeant, it's Pascal here. I'm over at Deasy's yard. I have a wounded suspect here on the floor. He needs an ambulance."

"Would that be the younger Geraghty by any chance? What ails him anyway?" Mulholland said.

"It would, Sarge, and he's been shot. He was threatening the life of a civilian, so I had to disable him in a hurry. I shot him in the knee."

"Good man, Pascal. That will be bloody sore for a while. Right. I'll get an ambulance out to you now. When they get there, you'll need to accompany the suspect back to the hospital in Galway to provide protection for the ambulance crew, and if there's any nonsense, shoot him in the other knee. We don't want this nasty bugger getting away again. Bring all the weapons with you in the ambulance, and I'll get forensics out to Deasy's. Tell them not to touch anything, and not to clean up – as if," Mulholland said.

The ambulance took nearly half an hour to get from Clifden to Deasy's yard on the outskirts of Roundstone. Geraghty was lucky. Brosnan had a very comprehensive first aid kit in the squad car, and was able to make the lad as comfortable as possible while they waited. He wrapped his knee in a pressure dressing; gave him some paracetamol for the pain, and covered him in a thermal blanket to stop hypothermia setting in following the shock.

All the while he was administering to Geraghty, the Deasys were offering unhelpful suggestions as to how they thought he should be treated.

* * *

When Séan Mulholland had finished summoning the ambulance and the forensic team, he called Hays to update him on the new developments.

"That's good news, Séan. Pascal did a fine job. Looks like we have them both sewn up nicely now. Any sign of the money?" Hays said.

"Oh, God, I never thought of that. It's probably in the car the younger one brought to Deasy's. I'd better get Jim Dolan out there to recover it and take statements from the Deasys too," Mulholland said.

Mulholland contacted Garda Jim Dolan on the radio. Dolan was down at Ferris's garage fuelling the squad car.

"Jim, it's Sergeant Mulholland. Can you get out to Tadgh Deasy's yard, pronto? One of the Geraghtys has turned up waving a loaded gun around. It's OK, Pascal has sorted him out, but the money from the Paddy McKeever robbery may be still in Geraghty's car, and we need to recover it before it disappears."

"Understood, Sergeant. I'm on my way," Dolan said, finishing up his business with the petrol station briskly and setting off out along the old bog road to Roundstone.

Dolan arrived out to Deasy's yard to find that the ambulance had departed with Geraghty and Brosnan. Brosnan's car was still in the yard, locked up, and the two Deasys were inside the house recovering from their ordeal.

Dolan knocked on the back door of the house.

"Yes, Guard, what can we do for you now?" Tadgh Deasy said as he answered the door.

"Can I come in, Mr Deasy? I need to take a statement from you and your son about the goings on here this morning."

"Ah, can ye not leave us in peace? We've both been nearly killed by that madman. It's like Dodge City round here these days," Deasy said, still blocking the door.

"It won't take long, Mr Deasy, and then we'll be done and can leave you alone," Dolan said, advancing into the doorway in a manner that indicated he was not to be put off.

Deasy reluctantly stood aside and let him into the kitchen of the house. The room was dark and smelled vaguely of cooked bacon and boiled cabbage. The bare wooden kitchen table had two large mugs and a milk carton on it, and what had been a packet of biscuits lying empty beside the sugar bowl. A single bare bulb suspended on a wire from the ceiling provided the only rather feeble illumination.

Ragged curtains drooped in front of the single dirty window, and a gas cooker caked in grease and black stains stood beside the earthenware sink that was piled high with dirty crockery.

Dolan sat down on one of the four bare wooden rail-backed chairs and took out his notepad.

The statements were written out longhand and read back to each of the men, who signed and dated them.

"Is that you done, so?" Tadgh Deasy said.

"Almost. I just want to have a look in this bag underneath the table," Dolan said, bending down to collect the item that Shay had hurriedly placed there while his father was obfuscating at the door earlier.

"You can't do that! You need a warrant," Shay said with some alarm in his voice.

"I don't think so, Shay. Probable cause and the proceeds of a crime. No warrant required."

Dolan lifted the bag onto the table and examined its contents.

"Looks like the money from the post office van robbery to me. What's it doing here?" Dolan asked.

"It was in the blue car yer man was driving," Tadgh Deasy said rather grumpily.

"And how did it find its way to underneath your kitchen table?" The Garda said.

Tadgh Deasy and his son exchanged worried glances.

"Eh, we took it in for safe keeping, didn't we? With the back window out of the car, anyone could have taken it. We were doing you lot a favour," the older Deasy said.

"Very thoughtful. I hope it's all here?" Dolan said.

"What! Are you accusing us of theft? And me nearly getting me head blown off by that scumbag!" Tadgh Deasy said.

"Take it easy, Tadgh. I'm not accusing anyone of anything – I just asked the question. Now, I'll be taking this in to the station in Clifden." Dolan stood up, clutching the plastic bag full of money tightly.

"I don't suppose there'll be any reward for finding the cash?" Shay said.

"Reward indeed. Be thankful I'm not doing you for handling stolen property," Dolan said, letting himself out of the old musty kitchen into the relative fresh air of the grimy yard.

When they heard Dolan's car leaving the yard, Tadgh said to his son who was looking a bit glum, "Could have been worse, lad. At least we got the fifteen hundred that they paid for the old jeep back!"

Chapter Twenty-four

At the Abbey Glen, Sinéad Loughran, the forensic team lead attached to the Galway Detective Unit, had arrived with two others. They made an odd picture strolling around in their white suits, examining the ground and taking what seemed like endless photographs from every possible angle.

Loughran approached Lyons as her two colleagues continued to gather evidence of the earlier events, removing her face mask and hood, allowing her blonde ponytail to fall down her back.

"Hi, Maureen. You two don't do things by halves, do you?" she said cheerfully.

"Tell me about it. Have you much more to do here?"

"No, we're just about done. There's not much for us here. The ARU guy says he discharged his weapon at the man believing he was about to kill Inspector Hays. The bullet went straight through the guy's shoulder – it's probably lodged in the undergrowth somewhere, but we don't need to find it anyway," Loughran said.

"Do you need to get a statement from Tom — that's his name, by the way."

"No, not when he's official ARU. They answer to a higher authority," Loughran said, rolling her eyes to heaven.

"When can we re-open the road? The hotel guests are getting restless," Lyons said.

"Give me another five minutes, then we'll leave you to it. Are you OK, Maureen?"

"I dunno, Sinéad. I think I might look for a job in admin after this. It wasn't nice," Lyons said.

"Not at all girl. You're a born thief taker — always will be. Go get yourself a strong drink and you'll be as right as rain by the afternoon." She leaned in and gave Lyons a hug, noting that she was beginning to well up.

* * *

As the forensic team packed up the tools of their trade, and Tom bid them goodbye, Hays and Lyons got back into the manager's Audi and reversed it back down the drive, bringing it to a halt outside the door of the hotel.

Lionel Wallace came trotting out as they got out of the car.

"Show's over, Mr Wallace. All done and dusted. The lodgement is safe and sound in the boot of your car, and you can tell the guests that the driveway is now re-opened. There's a fairly large patch of sawdust up near the gate where the gunman bled out a bit, but other than that, it's all as before," Hays said.

"Crikey. Was anyone killed?" Wallace said, his natural morbid curiosity getting the better of him.

"No, nothing so dramatic, though it was a close call. Inspector Hays nearly got it in the gut," Lyons said, recalling her own private horror as she watched Anselm Geraghty level his gun at her partner.

"Well, I'd better let the guests know that they can leave now, and then I'll be off to the bank. Do you think there's any more danger?" Wallace said.

"No, you should be fine now, but if you like we'll come as far as the bank with you just in case," Hays said.

"Oh, yes, thank you, that would be wonderful. Hold on here, I'll be back in a jiffy," Wallace said, disappearing back inside the luxurious lobby to give the all clear.

Moments later Wallace re-appeared at the door with a solemn procession of anxious guests trailing behind him towing their wheelie suitcases.

Hays drove behind the hotel manager's car into Clifden, and they waited in their own vehicle till he had disappeared inside holding his bag of money close to himself.

"You know, I'll bet he'll dine out on that story for years. Where to now?" Lyons said.

"Let's drop in to Séan on the way back. I could murder a cup of coffee, and I bet he has a brew going."

They drove the short distance out to Clifden Garda Station. Lyons felt that the place seemed so normal after the events of the morning. People were just going about their regular business, although the town was quiet, it being between Christmas and New Year.

"Ah, Inspectors, come in. I was just about to make a cup of tea. Will you join me?" Mulholland said as they entered the station.

Lyons and Hays exchanged an amused glance.

"Lovely, Séan, and you might have a little something to put in it – we've had a tough day," Hays said.

"Oh, right, of course. Come in and sit yourselves down while I get it ready."

A few minutes later and Séan Mulholland reappeared with a tray holding three good sized mugs, a large teapot, a carton of milk and a bottle of expensive whiskey. Hays picked up the bottle, and looked at the label.

"Wow, Séan, you're pushing the boat out a bit. This is good stuff."

"A present from a grateful customer, Inspector. His tractor was stolen a couple of weeks ago and we managed to get it back for him before it left the county. Almost brand new it was too. He was lucky, there's too much of that sort of thing going on round here these days. Some of those machines can be worth as much as twenty thousand euro you know," the sergeant said.

"Yes, I know. But I bet he had almost no security in place. The farmers give out about the rise and rise of rural crime, but they'd never think about doing anything for themselves to prevent it," Hays said.

Hays poured a generous tot of the amber liquid into all three mugs.

"So, I hear you got your man?" Mulholland said, keen to change the subject.

"Well, sort of. To be honest, if it wasn't for Tom from the ARU, I wouldn't be sitting here now. Those guys certainly seem to know what they're doing," Hays said.

"I never had much truck with them out here to be honest. But I've heard they can be handy enough. Oh, and by the way, Jim Dolan has recovered a good deal of the stolen money that they took off poor Paddy McKeever. It was found under the kitchen table at Tadgh Deasy's place after the younger Geraghty was carted off."

Hays raised an eyebrow.

"Do you think Deasy had anything to do with it?" Lyons asked.

"No, I don't think so. He says it was in the car young Geraghty was driving, and he took it into the house for safe keeping. I'm inclined to believe most of it. That kind of thing is way out of his league," Mulholland said.

"Still, he could have helped himself to a few bob and we'd never know," Lyons said.

"Maybe, but he's careful enough to keep on the right side of us. He knows we could make his life a misery if he stepped too far out of line," Mulholland said.

"Fair enough, and he was a bit out of pocket over the jeep after all, so probably best to let well alone. But get the local traders to keep an eye out all the same. If he did pocket some of the proceeds, we can't just let it go," Lyons said.

"Will do. Paddy McKeever's funeral is on tomorrow out in Roundstone. He was from there originally, and he still has a brother who works the land at the edge of the village. Will someone be out for it?" Mulholland said, changing the subject deftly.

"I'll talk to the Super, but I guess it will be us two again. Will it be a big affair?" Hays said.

"God, it will. He was very well liked and respected, and sure he knew everybody around. The church will be full. It's following ten o'clock mass, I'll be going in myself," Mulholland said.

They chatted on for a while about the events of the past week, and after a second cup of tea – this time without reinforcements – the two detectives left Clifden, saying that they would probably see Séan again tomorrow at the funeral.

* * *

On the way back to the city, the day had brightened up considerably. It was still cool, but the sun was breaking through in places, and the road had dried out, allowing Hays to maintain a good pace. Conversation inevitably turned to the events of the morning.

"Christ, Mick, what a day. Are you OK?" Lyons asked.

"Yeah, I wasn't too scared. I knew Tom and Ronan had me covered, but it wasn't nice. You?"

"A bit shook up, but I'll get over it. It wasn't nice seeing that gun aimed at your chest. And it was horrible because I couldn't do anything about it without making the situation worse for you."

Hays leaned across and squeezed her hand.

"And what was that business about Joey?" she said.

"Oh, that. I was puzzled myself at first, but now I remember. Joey Geraghty was a bad lad I was responsible for putting away about twenty years ago when I was a humble detective constable. It was that time when robbing post offices and cash in transit vans was all the rage. We nabbed Joey following a tip off when he was blagging a cash van. The driver got shot, but survived, and Geraghty got fifteen years for attempted murder. Then, about two years into his sentence, he was found dead on the floor of the toilets with his throat cut. He must have made a lot of enemies. Joey was Anselm's father," Hays said.

"Wow. Do you think they set out to trap you?"

"I doubt it. I'd say it was opportunist. But he knew who I was all the same. Anyway, he got his."

"That was some shot Tom took," Lyons said.

"Sure was. I talked to him after and he said it was a 'maximum debilitation, minimum lethal damage' shot. Bloody hell!" Hays said.

"Anyway, it did the trick, thank heavens," Lyons said.

"That reminds me, you'd better get your gun back from Pascal. Give him a call later and we can pick it up tomorrow. No doubt the lovely Inspector Nicholson will want to talk to him about shooting Geraghty in the knee," Hays said.

"Hmm. I hope he's up to dealing with that. He won't be used to being assumed to be in the wrong in that odd way that Nicholson works," Lyons said.

"Yeah, I think I'll step in and provide some support to him. It's not fair to hang him out to dry when he probably saved Deasy's life," Hays said.

"So, do you think we should go into Mill Street now?" Lyons said.

"I'd prefer to go home to be honest. I need to have a shower and relax for a few hours. Why don't I call the office and see if Plunkett is around? With a bit of luck, he'll be off for these few days, and if he's not there, we can bunk off too," Hays said.

Hays was correct. Superintendent Plunkett was available on an emergency basis only till next week – the first week of January.

"Excellent. Let's go home!" Lyons said.

Chapter Twenty-five

Paddy McKeever's funeral was, as Séan Mulholland had predicted, a large event in Roundstone. The weather was overcast and cold, with a stiff breeze blowing in from the Atlantic, but the rain appeared to be holding off – at least for the moment.

The Gardaí were represented in numbers, with Hays, Mulholland and Brosnan all in full uniform, and Lyons dressed in a neat navy suit with a smart white blouse beneath.

At the front of the church, Paddy's wife, Breeda, sat forlornly with their two daughters on one side, and Paddy's brother Tommy on the other with his wife and family. In the second pew, just behind the family, workmates from An Post in Galway along with a number of managers from the organisation, squeezed in.

The priest spoke eloquently about Paddy's years of service to the community, coming out in all weathers to deliver and collect the mail, and often bringing errands to some of the less able-bodied parishioners who were living in some of the very remote cottages out by the coast along what was now fashionably called the Wild Atlantic Way.

Tommy spoke from the altar of how Paddy had selflessly left the small family farm many years ago, realising that it was unable to sustain both brothers, and had gone to work in the city, where his sacrifice had been rewarded by his meeting with Breeda, and the wonderful happy life that they had had together, producing two lovely daughters, before he was so cruelly cut down. Tommy thanked the Gardaí for bringing the culprits to justice so quickly, and expressed his hope that they would be incarcerated for a very long time indeed.

The priest eventually brought proceeding to an end, advising the congregation that the family had extended an invitation to all present to join them in the Roundstone House Hotel for refreshments after the burial.

Paddy McKeever was wheeled slowly out of the church, and as he was being manhandled into the hearse for the short journey to the local graveyard, Ivan, Paddy's nephew, opened the boot of his car and served generous glasses of whiskey to the mourners, in time honoured fashion, "just to keep out the cold".

The funeral procession made its way slowly from the church, out along the old bog road for about a mile, before turning down towards Gurteen Bay, and the graveyard that stood on the high ground between the Gurteen and Dog's Bay beaches. As Lyons walked along sombrely behind the slow-moving hearse, she couldn't help but recall the last time she had visited that same graveyard when Oliver Weldon had been discovered, alive, in a freshly dug grave during the pony show murder that they had solved the previous year.

As Paddy's coffin was lowered into the rocky earth, the sunshine finally gave in to a blustery shower. The priest invited the mourners to recite a decade of the rosary as a final farewell to their friend and loved one, and the grave was covered over before several wreaths were placed on top.

Hays left Séan Mulholland to represent the Gardaí at the hotel, while he and Lyons set off with Pascal Brosnan to the young Garda's house to retrieve Lyons' weapon.

"We won't keep you long, Pascal, you'll want to be joining the rest of them in town, but we need to get Maureen's gun back and hand it in," Hays said.

"Will there be any bother over the shooting? After all, the gun wasn't even assigned to me," Brosnan said as they entered his neat detached bungalow situated just a few hundred metres from the one-man Garda station in Roundstone.

"I was going to talk to you about that. Inspector Lyons has been getting a bit of heat from Internal Affairs over the shot she fired at the departing jeep the day I got hit in the leg, so you can expect a visit from an Inspector Nicholson at some stage, unless we can head him off," Hays said.

Brosnan collected the pistol from the locked gun safe he had in his kitchen, and gave it to Maureen Lyons. Lyons counted the bullets, confirming that just one had been used, and ensured that the magazine was removed and the chamber emptied before placing it on the table.

"I lifted the spent bullet case off the floor of the yard too, Inspector," Brosnan said, producing the shiny brass item from his jacket pocket.

"Good man, Pascal. It all helps," she said.

"So, this is what we're going to do, Pascal. If you get a call from Nicholson, or anyone else from IA, let me know at once, and set up the meeting for a day or two after the call. I'll come out, and we can do the interview together. That way I can cover your back, and make sure he goes away with nothing. Be sure to tell Séan of our plan to keep him in the picture," Hays said.

"There's nothing in it anyway. If I hadn't fired at Geraghty, we'd be going to Shay Deasy's funeral tomorrow, plain and simple. I don't see why we have to be so defensive about it," Brosnan said, rather annoyed.

"Easy, Pascal. No one is saying you didn't do exactly the right thing, but these IA boys have their job to do too. They are very often officers who had some issues or just couldn't cut it in the front line, so they have a chip on both shoulders. And I know Nicholson – he can be slippery enough, so just go with the flow and let me deal with anything awkward if it arises. Have you written up a report of the incident yet?" Hays asked.

"Not yet. Séan wants it in by tomorrow."

"Right. Well do yourself a favour. Email it to me first before you file it. It's not so much what is said in these reports, as *how* it is said that counts. Put plenty of emphasis on the unstable state of the gunman, the unpredictability of his actions, that sort of thing. If it needs a bit of tweaking, I'll polish it up a bit. Is that OK?" Hays said.

"Yes, thanks, that would be great. I'm not that good with these reports and the like," Brosnan said.

"Good man. Now, away with you to the hotel, and let us get back into town before the weather really sets in."

* * *

169

Lyons and Hays got back into Mill Street Garda Station soon after lunch. There were mounds of paperwork to be generated around the entire episode, and they both spent the afternoon writing it up in their respective computer systems.

Lyons took both Sig Sauer P220s back to the armoury and signed them back in. The officer noted that two bullets had been fired, and reminded her that a full report would have to be completed and filed before the week was out.

As she continued with the boring job of typing up the long and detailed account of the original crime, and the subsequent pursuit of the Geraghtys, she tuned into Galway FM radio, where news of the events of the day were making headlines. A member of the Garda press office was on the case, and told a convincing tale of how the two criminals had finally been run to earth and apprehended through the bravery of a crack team of detectives and other officers from the Galway station.

They had managed to get a taped interview with Lionel Wallace as well, and he was obviously enjoying the limelight, and dramatized the whole thing like an episode of EastEnders, much to the delight of the journalist involved.

Chapter Twenty-six

It was the first week of January, and things were slowly returning to whatever 'normal' was in the headquarters of the Galway Detective Unit. The Geraghtys remained under close arrest at the hospital, and would be taken, as soon as they were sufficiently mobile, before a judge where they would inevitably be held on remand while the Gardaí prepared their book of evidence.

Hays had arranged a meeting with Superintendent Plunkett for eleven o'clock, and at quarter to the hour, he walked into Lyons' office.

"I'm going up to see himself in a few minutes. Is there anything we need to watch out for?" Hays said.

"Nothing special, Mick. Just see if you can find out what IA have said and if there's anything coming at us from that quarter," Lyons said.

"Righto. I'd forgotten about the fragrant Inspector Nicholson. And I never heard anything from Pascal about an interview either. I'll ask himself what the story is. See you later," Hays said, and disappeared upstairs.

"Come in, Mick. Happy New Year to you," said Finbarr Plunkett, obviously in a cheerful mood.

"Thanks, sir, many happy returns."

"Coffee?"

"No thanks, sir, I've just had one downstairs. Did you have a good break, sir?" Hays said.

"Well, a good bit better than yours, that's for sure. That was a bad business with those two lads. Are we sound for a conviction?" the superintendent said.

"We will be. We should have enough to get them life anyway, at least the older one. Young Emmet may get away with ten or twelve if he has a good brief," Hays said.

"We'll try and get them up before Judge Meehan. He has very little sympathy for those types, and if he's doing it, I can have a word in his ear in advance," Plunkett said.

"Good idea, sir. So, what's on the agenda for now?" Hays said.

"We need to get moving on our new plans now that we're into the new year. You'd be surprised how time goes by with these things. Have you figured out how you want to arrange things yet?"

"More or less. I still have to talk to Eamon Flynn, but that apart, I think I have everything more or less ready to go. I haven't heard from the OPW yet though. Have you?" Hays said.

"Not at all, dozy lot. I'll get someone to give them a nudge this week. I'll need you to set aside a couple of hours for me later in the week to start work on the budgets, shall we say Thursday afternoon?" Plunkett said.

"Yes, Thursday should be fine. By the way, did you hear anything from Internal Affairs? Nicholson should have written his report by now."

"No, no I didn't, now that you mention it. I think I'll give the chief a call later on. A sort of pre-emptive strike, if you know what I mean," Plunkett said.

"Good idea. Inspector Lyons is a bit anxious until it's all cleared up."

"OK. Well I'll let you know if I find out anything. I wouldn't be too concerned if I was her. Once the final outcome was positive, they might huff and puff a bit, but I doubt if it will lead to anything."

"Thanks, sir. Will that be all?" Hays said.

"Yes, Mick. See you Thursday. Thanks."

* * *

When Hays had left to go upstairs, Lyons was still working on the seemingly endless paperwork associated with the Geraghtys when her phone rang.

"Hi, Maureen. It's Sinéad. Look, this may be something and nothing, but I thought I'd give you a call all the same," the forensic team lead said.

"Sounds ominous, Sinéad. What's up?"

"Well, an ambulance crew were called out to a deceased in one of the yards down by the docks this morning. Some rough sleeper succumbed to the frost and apparently died of hypothermia. But they found a Post-it Note stuck to the front of his coat with just two letters written in pencil on it, and they called it in as being potentially suspicious," Sinéad said.

"Oh? And what were the two letters?"

"A.G. Doesn't mean anything to me, but it is a bit odd, so we went down to take a look. There's no sign of any kind of attack or anything, it just looks like the man died from exposure. He was in poor condition anyway," Sinéad said.

"Any idea who he was? Any I.D.?"

"Nothing on him, but a couple of other rough sleepers turned up when they saw the ambulance, and someone said his name was 'Rollo'," Sinéad said.

"Shit! He's one of Mick's snouts. He gave us some information about the Geraghtys just before Christmas. Are you sure there's no sign of foul play? The older Geraghty brother is called Anselm – A.G."

"Wow. Well in that case I'll have a good thorough look around, and I'll get Dr Dodd out and he can do a PM on the poor old fella too. Do you want to come down?"

"Yes. I'll get Mick and we'll be down in a few minutes. Mick is just upstairs at the moment, but he won't be long. Where exactly is it?" Lyons said.

"It's the fuel depot – McIntyre's – on the east side of the harbour. I'll preserve the area till you get here."

"Great. See you soon."

* * *

It was a wretched scene down at McIntyre's fuel depot where Rollo had been found. Amongst the piles of peat briquettes, bags of smokeless coal, and sacks of logs, partly covered with a dirty green tarpaulin, the lifeless body of the old man, still wrapped in his filthy old herringbone tweed coat, lay in the dirt.

Hays donned a pair of blue vinyl gloves and went carefully through the pockets of the old man's coat. In the inside pocket of the jacket, he found a naggin bottle of whiskey with about a tablespoon full of amber liquid left in the bottom. He lifted it carefully out and handed it to Sinéad.

"Have this analysed, will you, Sinéad?" Hays said handing her the bottle.

In another pocket, Hays discovered a ten and a five euro note, and three more euro in coins. He lifted the money carefully, and placed it in a plastic evidence bag.

As Hays straightened up, the figure of Dr Julian Dodd, dressed immaculately as ever, loomed into sight.

"Good morning Inspector, Maureen, Sinéad. What am I doing here?" the doctor said.

"This is Rollo," Hays said, indicating the prone figure of the dead man on the ground. "There are some aspects of his death that may be suspicious, so we need you to have a look, and then do a PM to see what took him," Hays said.

"You're joking! Two or three of these old guys die out here every week. What makes you think this one is a bit off?" the doctor said.

Lyons explained the note they had found stuck to Rollo's coat, and the tentative connection to the Geraghtys.

"Very well. If you insist, Inspector. Can we get him out of this dreadful place?"

"Yes, sure. Give me a call later when you have some news."

As Rollo was loaded up into the anonymous black Mercedes van, Lyons turned to Hays.

"I'm really sorry, Mick. I know you had known him a long time. Are you OK?" she said.

"Yeah, I'm fine. He wasn't a bad old bugger you know. I realise we didn't move in the same social circles, but still."

"Yeah, I know. Never mind. If there's anything iffy about it, Dodd will find it, don't worry."

Chapter Twenty-seven

Superintendent Finbarr Plunkett's secretary put the call to the chief superintendent through to him.

"Good afternoon, Chief Superintendent. Thanks for taking the call. I just wanted to have a quick word with you about the Internal Affairs enquiry into Inspector Lyons' use of a firearm," Plunkett said.

"Oh, yes, Finbarr. Hold on, I have the draft report here somewhere. I was looking at it yesterday," the chief said.

"Yes, here it is. Let me see. Well, Inspector Nicholson has formed the view that Lyons discharged her gun unnecessarily, but that in doing so, she did not endanger life. He recommends some re-training for her in the use of firearms and a note on her file. Is that how you see it, Finbarr?" the chief superintendent said.

"Well, not exactly, sir. It's clear to me that she felt her life, and that of her colleague, were directly threatened, and she discharged the weapon in an effort – successful as it turned out – to deter the gunman from firing again. We must remember that these two lads had already shot and wounded an officer. I'd be happy to leave it at that, but of course, I'll be guided by you, sir," Plunkett said.

"Hmm, I see what you mean. It might be best if we could play it down a bit, in view of the upcoming changes in the structure out there all right. Are you happy that this Inspector Lyons isn't a hot-head?" the chief superintendent said.

"Oh, she's anything but that, sir. She has been very successful in apprehending a number of very serious criminals over the past few years, and she's known for keeping a cool head. Even when she was taken captive by a nasty thug a couple of years ago, she stayed cool, and not only made her escape, but arrested the blighter while she was at it," Plunkett said, hoping he wasn't talking Lyons up too much.

"OK. Well, look, I'll have another word with Nicholson, see if he can tone it down a bit. I have a good bit of influence with that particular gentleman as it happens, so leave it with me."

"Thanks, sir. That would be very helpful. Oh, and Happy New Year, sir."

"What? Oh, yes, thanks. And will you have a word with Ms Lyons and suggest that she acts a little less like Annie bloody Oakley next time she has a gun in her hand?"

"Yes, sir, of course sir. All the best," Plunkett said, hanging up.

When Superintendent Plunkett had finished the call, he sent for Lyons who was back in the station after the grim discovery down at the docks.

"Come in, Maureen. Take a seat. I've just been speaking to the chief superintendent about Inspector Nicholson's report," he said, plonking himself back into his own chair.

"Oh, right. Am I in trouble?" she said.

"I don't think so. I explained to the chief that you were not given to rash behaviour, and that you genuinely felt that your life, and the life of Hays was under threat. Nicholson of course wants you to be re-trained, and all sorts, but I think I managed to talk the chief around."

"So, what happens now, sir?"

"Probably nothing. I doubt we'll hear any more about it. The chief won't come back to me unless it's being taken further, and from what he said, I think that's very unlikely. How's Mick's leg coming along?" Plunkett said.

"He's fine. You'd hardly notice anything now, although it doesn't stop him putting on the agony act if he thinks he's not getting enough attention from me."

"In other words, he's a typical man, Maureen," Plunkett said with a smile.

"I'm glad you said that, sir. I couldn't possibly comment! Will there be a note on my record sir, about the gun I mean?"

"I'll check it in a month or so, but I don't expect there will, no."

"Thank you, sir. Is that all?" she said.

"Yes, that's it. I'll let you get back to it."

* * *

It was late afternoon by the time Sinéad Loughran called Hays about the death of Rollo.

"Hi, Inspector. We have some results now from the man we brought in earlier – Rollo, is it?"

"Yes, that's him. What's the story?" Hays said.

"It looks as if the bottle he was drinking from was heavily laced with methyl alcohol. He probably wouldn't have noticed it very much – the flavour would have been disguised by the whiskey. He probably thought it was just a very strong bottle. So, what with his general condition, and the adulteration of the booze, his constitution just gave up. He died of heart failure. I'm sorry, sir," Loughran said.

"I see. Any idea of the time of death, Sinéad?"

"Dr Dodd says probably between 2 and 5 a.m. It's hard to be more accurate, but body temperature supports that estimate," Loughran said.

"Are there any fingerprints, DNA or other trace evidence anywhere on his clothes, or in the yard?" Hays asked.

"Nothing, sir. The bottle is clean except for his own dabs, and the yard is wet and dirty, so there's no discernible footprints of any use. There are no other traces on the man's clothes either."

"I don't suppose there's any CCTV in the yard?" Hays said.

"No, sir. Nothing anywhere near there I'm afraid."

"Damn. Poor guy didn't stand a chance really. What happens to these people when they pass like this, Sinéad?" Hays asked.

"I think the council arranges something for them, sir, but I'll check it up and let you know."

"OK, thanks Sinéad. Talk later."

Lyons came into the office just as Hays was finishing the call.

"What's the story?" she asked.

Hays relayed the information that Sinéad Loughran had provided.

"I'm sorry, Mick. That's lousy. Do you think we should open another murder enquiry?" Lyons asked.

"I have an idea. Get Eamon to ask around amongst the other rough sleepers. I doubt that he'll come up with anything, but you never know. Then I'll contact the council and see if we can arrange some sort of proper funeral for Rollo. That might bring out a bit more information. Nothing too fancy that would make his mates feel uncomfortable – maybe some kind of buffet with soup and sandwiches in the grounds of the church."

"Good idea. But do we need a board and an incident room set up?" Lyons asked.

"No, I don't think so, not yet anyway. I'll have a word upstairs, but in the way of these things, with no evidence that we can see, I doubt if they'll want to spend a lot of time on it to be honest," Hays said.

"That's a bit harsh, isn't it?" Lyons said.

"It's just being realistic, Maureen. It'll probably be put down to sudden death due to exposure. Unfortunately, the likes of Rollo don't vote, and don't pay taxes," Hays said.

"Terrific," she said and went to find Eamon.

* * *

Hays waited till his meeting with the superintendent on Thursday to raise the issue of Rollo's death. There was no hurry – after all Rollo wasn't going anywhere, and it was not as if there were queues of grieving relatives waiting to bury the poor man.

Eamon Flynn's investigations among the underprivileged of Galway city had revealed nothing. These men were suspicious of the Gardaí who rarely wanted to do anything useful for them, and more often than not just wanted to move them on, or even prosecute them for vagrancy, or some of the petty theft that they indulged in to stay alive. Flynn's manner didn't help either. He didn't want to be amongst them, and his hostility was quickly picked up by men who relied on their instincts for survival.

On Thursday afternoon Hays kept his appointment with the superintendent. They spent an hour going through a series of spreadsheets covering everything from overtime and allowances for all the members of the force under Plunkett's control, to stationery and fuel costs for the plethora of vehicles under their management. As they completed the last of them, Plunkett said, "You've no idea how happy I am to be handing this lot over to you, Mick. They drive me round the bend."

"It will take me a while to get the hang of it all, sir," Hays said.

"Ah, you'll be fine. To be honest, I doubt if anyone actually looks at them in any case!"

"You heard about my snout, Rollo, I suppose, sir?" Hays said, keen to get off the topic of budgets.

"I did, Mick. Is there something more I should know?" Plunkett said.

Hays went on to explain about the lethal cocktail they had discovered in Rollo's whiskey bottle, and the Post-it Note stuck to his overcoat.

"Is that all you've got, Mick?" Plunkett said.

"Yes. That's about it. None of his contemporaries are saying anything, and there's bugger all evidence, although I'm sure the Geraghtys had a hand in it somehow, even though they were locked up at the time."

"Ah, Mick, if I were you I'd leave it alone. What good will it do spending scarce resources running around after a down and out, even if he was helpful to us from time to time? We've more to be doing with our time," Plunkett said.

While Hays recognised the reality of what Plunkett was saying, he didn't entirely like it. In a funny way, he had been fond of the old guy, and he'd known him for a good few years. But he also knew that these folks rarely got any of the right kind of attention from the authorities. They were a nuisance to be tolerated rather than looked after, and what had happened to Rollo probably wasn't all that unusual in any case. He filed it away, as he had done a number of times in the past.

* * *

As soon as the Geraghtys were fit to walk around, they were taken before the court for a brief hearing. Hays went along to ensure that there was no possible chance of them getting bail and he wasn't disappointed. Judge Meehan remanded them to appear in Loughrea in two weeks' time, and while the judge looked curiously at their injuries, he made no comment.

As they were being taken out of the courthouse to the waiting transport that would remove them to the remand centre in Claremorris, Hays encountered the two brothers being walked out, handcuffed, in the company of two armed Gardaí.

"I'll be seeing you later, Mr Hays," Anselm Geraghty said with a sneer on his face, "oh, and give my regards to Rollo."

Chapter Twenty-eight

"You know what you need, Ms Lyons?" Hays said to his partner back at the station.

"And what would that be, Mr Hays?" she replied with an impish grin on her face.

"A holiday! Why don't we see if we can get away for a week to somewhere nice? Then, when we get back, we can start working on the superintendent's master plan," Hays said.

"Sounds good to me. Are you thinking bikinis or winter warmers?" she said.

"Bikini – definitely, and speedos for me, of course."

"Bloody hell, Mick. That's a scary mental image for a girl at this hour of the morning. Canaries?"

"Perfect. I'll square it with upstairs, and you get onto the travel agent and see what you can conjure up. My treat, so go easy on the credit card, there's plenty of budget accommodation to be had, even at this time of year," he said.

"No chance. I'm a five-star sort of girl, or hadn't you noticed?" she said, smiling warmly at him, and thinking how thoughtful he was.

* * *

When Hays returned from a brief chat with Superintendent Plunkett, he popped into Lyons' office.

"How does Los Cristianos in Tenerife grab you? Leaving Sunday morning from Shannon," she said.

"Terrific. Well done you, and the boss thought it was an excellent idea too, by the way."

"Just as long as he's not coming with us!" Lyons said.

"Well, I did invite him, but he says he's too busy!"

* * *

The two detectives enjoyed a glorious week in the Canary Islands. While Hays' leg hadn't enjoyed four hours sitting in the middle seat of three on the somewhat cramped Ryanair Boeing 737, once they disembarked, and he got a chance to stretch it on the long walk to collect their baggage, it eased out and felt a lot better.

Lyons had chosen the hotel well. It was the height of luxury, and positioned conveniently close to the beach and the centre of the little resort, which seemed to have a good array of excellent restaurants, bars and shops.

The weather was kind to them too. At between twenty-three and twenty-seven degrees and sunny each day, it was just the type of climate they both enjoyed.

They spent most days lounging by the pool or swimming in the sea, and while Hays was still careful not to walk too far, they managed a few gentle strolls along the coast on top of the dramatic cliffs that give Los Cristianos its unique scenery.

In the evenings, they enjoyed some excellent meals at any one of the seafood restaurants in the town, and after a nice bottle of good red Spanish wine, they ambled back to their hotel, retired, and made love gently and passionately in the enormous king-sized bed.

By the end of the week, they were both feeling thoroughly refreshed and were almost looking forward to getting back to work. Hays' leg had healed up well by this time, and the journey back didn't bother him nearly as much.

Arriving back into Shannon at almost midnight, the weather had taken a turn for the worse, and flurries of light snow were drifting across the apron at the airport, but not sticking for long, as the temperature was just above four degrees.

When they saw it, they both decided to check in to a local hotel for the night rather than drive back to Galway.

"Let's finish off the week in style, Maureen," Hays said as they checked into the Park Inn just near the airport.

"Amen to that!" Lyons echoed with a wide grin on her pretty face.

* * *

Several months later, when the Geraghtys' case finally got to court, the case was concluded pretty quickly. They pleaded guilty to a number of the charges against them, but not guilty to the murder of Paddy McKeever. But the evidence told a different story, and with the fingerprints on the spent cartridge, and positive evidence that Anselm's gun had been used to fire the fatal shot, with his fingerprints all over it, there was little doubt. The jury took just two hours with their deliberations, and convicted them both of murder, aggravated assault, robbery, and wounding a police officer in the execution of his duty.

Mitigation was entered by the defence for Emmet Geraghty. It was put forward that he was being led and coerced by his older brother, and that he was scared what would happen if he didn't go along with him. This was largely shot down by the prosecution, citing the incident at Deasy's yard, where Emmet, acting alone, had threatened the lives of both Tadgh and Shay Deasy.

Both were handed down life sentences, with the judge specifying that Anselm should not be eligible for parole for eighteen years.

Just over a year into his sentence, Anselm Geraghty was discovered at 6 a.m. lying in a pool of his own blood on the cold, wet floor of the toilet block in Limerick prison. The prison authorities reported he had been stabbed with a finely sharpened tooth brush handle that had been found lodged in his carotid artery.

When Hays heard about the incident, he said to Lyons, "Some of those old lags have very long memories. The Geraghtys weren't much liked, even amongst the criminal fraternity. I'm not surprised, to be honest."

"It's a good job you can only die once," she said.

"How do you mean?" Hays said.

"Well, we know there were at least two deaths down to him – McKeever and Rollo, and maybe more that we don't know about. What about Emmet Geraghty?"

"That's a funny thing. When he heard about his brother's death, he went completely mad. Literally mad. He was screaming and banging his head off the walls, and throwing himself about. They had to sedate him, but when it wore off, he was back at it again. Apparently he's being moved to that place in Dundrum where they keep the criminally insane. I doubt if he'll ever get out of there," Hays said.

"Good enough for them both, if you ask me. We don't need those types in our community."

* * *

Some months after the terrible events that led to the death of her husband, Breeda McKeever received a generous settlement from An Post, and a good pension to boot. But her heart never mended. Paddy had been her first, and only love, and his loss was almost too much to bear for the poor woman.

The benefits people worked hard with the management of An Post to encourage their customers to have their weekly allowances paid directly into bank accounts, so that large quantities of cash did not have to be transported on quiet country roads. This was quite successful, so that mounting any further armed robberies on An Post vans became a waste of time and too risky for the criminal community, given the poor returns.

A small cross was erected at the side of the road at Dog's Bay where Paddy had given his life in the cause of his work, and there were almost always fresh flowers propped up against it, no matter what the time of year, or the weather, although no one really knew where they came from.

When Hays and Lyons were back in harness in Mill Street, during a quiet moment in the office, Hays said, "It's going to be quite different with me taking up the new role as Superintendent you know."

"I know it is, and I'm still not sure that I'll be able to step into your shoes completely successfully," Lyons said.

"I know you'll probably do things quite differently to me, Maureen, but that doesn't mean you won't be just as effective. I've tried to observe your work objectively over the past while, and to be brutally honest, I think you'll do an even better job than me. Your instincts are sharper than mine, and you don't mind taking the odd risk to get the job done. That's a pretty heady mix. I'd say the criminal element in Galway is in some bother," Hays said.

"It's good of you to say so, Mick. Let's just hope it all works out. Oh, and does this mean you'll be chasing me around for all sorts of ridiculous reports every month, and giving out shite when I overspend on some vital thief taking operation?"

"Of course! And don't expect any sympathy, just because we're partners either," he said, smiling.

"Oh, don't worry, Mick, I have a few ways of sorting that out, wait till you see."

"And that would be?"

"All in good time – patience, dear man, patience!"

Character list

Senior Inspector Michael Hays – a tough, experienced Garda who has ambitions to progress his career either at home, or in a UK police force.

Inspector Maureen Lyons – a sassy policewoman who has a long track record of success due to her cunning ways and no-nonsense approach to policing.

Superintendent Finbarr Plunkett – a wily old Garda who keeps the Detective Unit under close observation and helps them deal with the ever-increasing bureaucracy.

Detective Sergeant Eamon Flynn – a determined and thorough member of the Detective Unit who is known for his persistence in pursuing wrong-doers.

Detective Sally Fahy – joined the Gardaí after a spell as a civilian worker with the force, this pretty blonde officer is going places.

Garda John O'Connor – loves nothing more than hacking into a criminal's laptop or mobile phone to reveal all those hidden secrets.

Sinéad Loughran – leads the forensic team attached to the Detective Unit to gather evidence and assist in successful prosecutions.

Dr Julian Dodd – the diminutive and sarcastic pathologist with a great nose for something out of place.

Sergeant Séan Mulholland – in charge of the Clifden Garda Station, and nearing retirement, Mulholland likes to take it easy, but can be very effective when things turn nasty.

Garda Jim Dolan – Mulholland's right-hand man in Clifden.

Garda Pascal Brosnan – runs the little Garda station in Roundstone single-handedly. His firearms training comes in useful from time to time.

Garda Peadar Tobin – another of Mulholland's men from the Clifden Station.

Inspector Jim Nicholson – works for the Garda's Internal Affairs department where he seeks out deviations from proper procedure.

Paddy McKeever – a much liked postman who delivers mail between Galway and Clifden.

Breeda McKeever – Paddy McKeever's wife.

Anselm Geraghty – a hardened criminal who seems to have a reckless streak.

Emmet Geraghty – Anselm's young brother – an equally vicious thug.

Rollo – a near down and out who mixes among the seedier citizens of Galway.

Sheila Bourke – Maureen Lyons' married sister who lives on what had been the family farm out near Athenry.

Séamus Bourke – Sheila's husband.

Lionel Wallace – the manager of the luxurious Abbey Glen Hotel.

Bridget O'Toole – the elderly post mistress who has been running the Post Office in Clifden for many years.

Aoife O'Toole – the post mistress's daughter who works in a nearby pharmacy.

Tadgh Deasy – an erstwhile car dealer and mechanic who is well known to the Gardaí.

Shay Deasy – Tadgh's son.

Tommy McKeever – Paddy McKeever's brother.

Ivan McKeever – Paddy McKeever's nephew.

Jean – paramedic.

Dr Brady – the local medical man from Roundstone.

Agnes – Dr Brady's nurse.

Mr Michael O'Flaherty – a competent surgeon based in Galway's Regional Hospital.

If you enjoyed this book, please let others know by leaving a quick review on Amazon. Also, if you spot anything untoward in the paperback, get in touch. We strive for the best quality and appreciate reader feedback.

editor@thebookfolks.com

www.thebookfolks.com

BOOKS BY DAVID PEARSON

In this series:

Murder on the Old Bog Road (Book 1)
Murder at the Old Cottage (Book 2)
Murder on the West Coast (Book 3)
Murder at the Pony Show (Book 4)
Murder on Pay Day (Book 5)
Murder in the Air (Book 6)
Murder at the Holiday Home (Book 7)
Murder on the Peninsula (Book 8)
Murder at the Races (Book 9)
Murder in a Safe Haven (Book 10)
Murder in an Irish Bog (Book 11)
Murder in a Seaside Town (Book 12)

In the Dublin Homicides series:

A Deadly Dividend
A Fatal Liaison
The China Chapter
Lethal in Small Doses

THE DUBLIN HOMICIDES SERIES:

Two very different police officers work together to solve cases in this mystery series with a cozy feel.

For Detective Inspector Aidan Burke, policing Dublin's streets is a duty, but protecting his officers comes first. That provides a good environment for promising detectives like DS Fiona Moore to grow. As this series of murder mysteries set in the metropolitan but at times parochial city and its surroundings progresses, we see Moore tackle difficult and dangerous cases with a good success rate. As Burke himself rises in rank, they become a formidable crime fighting duo.

All four books are free with Kindle Unlimited and available in paperback.

Made in United States
North Haven, CT
27 June 2022

20663862R00125